Destiny stared up at [ ] glassy, her chest mov[ ]

He gently pulled down the neck of her sweatshirt. His curved fangs made a wet *slick* sound as they slid down from his gums.

Finally, he could resist no longer. He lowered his head and licked her neck. Licked it, his rough tongue scraping over the soft skin. Licked it hungrily.

Then he opened his mouth wide and with a groan from deep in his gut, brought the fangs down. Pierced the pale skin. Sank the sharp fangs deep into her throat.

And began to drink.

Dangerous Girls

A novel by
R.L. STINE

Avon Books
An Imprint of HarperCollinsPublishers
Parachute

Library of Congress Cataloging-in-Publication Data
Stine, R.L.
Dangerous girls / R.L. Stine.
p. cm.
"A Parachute Press Book."
Summary: After sixteen-year-old Destiny and her twin sister,
Livvy, are turned into partial vampires at a summer camp, they
try to find the "Restorer," someone who can return them to
normal.
ISBN 0-06-053080-4 — ISBN 0-06-053081-2 (lib. bdg.)
ISBN 0-06-053082-0 (pbk.)
[1. Vampires—Fiction. 2. Sisters—Fiction. 3. Twins—Fiction.]
I. Title.
PZ7.S86037 Dan 2003   2003004101
[Fic]—dc21   CIP
                                                           AC

First Avon edition, 2004

AVON TRADEMARK REG. U.S. PAT. OFF. AND IN OTHER COUNTRIES,
MARCA REGISTRADA, HECHO EN U.S.A.
❖
Visit us on the World Wide Web!
www.harperteen.com

For Robert O. Warren,
who always asks the right questions,
even if I don't always have the right answers!

Contents

Part One

Part Two

Part Three

Part One

Chapter One
The Most Dangerous Day

*S*ummer *can't* be over already. Do I really have to leave Camp Blue Moon?

That's what Destiny Weller was thinking on the day she started to become a vampire.

She watched the yellow bus rumble away, carrying the last of the campers with it. The bus bounced over the narrow dirt road, then turned and disappeared into the trees.

"Hey, we're free!" someone yelled. "The little animals are gone!"

"Party time!"

"Who has car keys? Can we get a keg? Can we at least get some six-packs?"

A red afternoon sun was sinking behind the trees. The air suddenly carried a chill, a hint that summer was nearly over.

Destiny turned and searched for her sister, Livvy. The counselors gathered around the grassy hill that overlooked the road, laughing and joking, hugging each other, celebrating the end of the camp season.

She spotted Livvy in a circle of girls clustered around Renz. He was flirting with them, hugging them one by one. All the girls adored Renz, and why not?

He was so good-looking, tall and tanned, with that wavy, black hair, those dark, bedroom eyes—devilish eyes—that irresistible smile. So charming and funny and . . . grown-up.

Not like the other guys in camp, Destiny thought. Not like the counselors and junior counselors whose idea of a good time was going skinny-dipping in the lake after lights-out, or putting snakes in each other's beds.

Renz was too sophisticated for that.

Destiny didn't really know much about him. She knew that his real name was Lorenzo Angelini, and he had just a hint of an Italian accent, which made him even sexier. He had been hired as head waterfront counselor. But when Uncle Bob, the owner of Camp Blue Moon, suddenly took sick just before the kids arrived, Renz became head counselor.

"I see who you're staring at." Nakeisha Johnson came up behind Destiny and grabbed her shoulders, startling her.

Destiny laughed. "He's looking good in those tennis whites, isn't he!"

"Summer's too short," Nakeisha said. "Think I could follow him home? Maybe he'll adopt me."

"Actually, I'm watching my sister," Destiny said. "Do you believe those short shorts? You can see half her butt."

Nakeisha gazed at the crowd of girls around Renz. "Well don't turn green or anything. You know you're jealous. Renz spent so much time with Livvy."

"*All* the guys spent time with Livvy," Destiny replied. She watched Renz give Livvy a farewell hug, holding her close, his hands all over her bare back.

"Stop shaking your head," Nakeisha said. "How can identical twins be so different?"

"I told you. We're fraternal. Not identical," Destiny said.

"Oh. Right. Well, that explains it," Nakeisha replied, rolling her eyes.

"I'm fifteen minutes older," Destiny said. "See. I've got to act like the older sister."

A yellow jacket buzzed around them.

Destiny swatted it away. High in the darkening sky, a flock of honking geese flew in perfect V-formation, making its way from Canada. On the road below, the camp station wagon sped past, tires spinning up dust, jammed with counselors heading to town to buy beer.

"Everyone's acting happy, but this is so sad," Nakeisha said. "Tomorrow we'll all go our separate ways. I won't see you anymore." She turned and wrapped Destiny in a hug.

Destiny hugged her back. "You've been such a good friend. I really am going to miss you."

Both girls had tears in their eyes.

"At least you're going home to New York," Destiny said, letting go. She ran a hand through her short, straight blond hair. "Not boring little Dark Springs, Mass."

Nakeisha wiped tear stains off her cheeks. "I just got something in my eye, that's all. It's not like I hate saying good-bye or anything. You've got my e-mail address, right? And my cell number?"

Destiny nodded. "We can Instant Message each other."

"Maybe you can come to New York for Thanksgiving?"

Destiny laughed. "Yeah, if I win the lottery or something."

"Hey, know what? I'll be doing college visits in September and October. I know I'll be in Boston. Maybe I can come through Dark Springs."

"Excellent!" Destiny said. Over Nakeisha's shoulder, she saw Livvy, cigarette in hand, lip-locked with Cory Field, one of her many admirers. His arm around her shoulders, Cory began to lead Livvy toward the trees by the lake.

"Livvy—wait!" Destiny shouted. She took off running. "Hey, Liv—stop!"

Her sister turned and took a long drag on the cigarette. Cory kept his arm around her. "Hi, Dee. What's up?" Livvy asked.

"How's it going?" Cory said. "Pretty quiet without the kids, huh?"

Destiny nodded. "Liv, you haven't started packing," she said.

"Yeah, I know."

Destiny stared at her sister. Livvy did everything she could to look different from her twin. Destiny wore her hair short, so Livvy kept hers long, letting it flow down over her shoulders. Destiny hardly ever wore makeup, just a little blush and lip gloss from time to time. Livvy liked purple or dark red lipstick, and her biggest suitcase this summer had been filled with eye makeup.

Livvy had one nostril pierced, usually wore three different earrings in each ear, and loved to wear rings on every finger. She wanted to get a butterfly tattoo on her shoulder, but held off, knowing her dad would give her all kinds of grief.

Destiny would never admit it to anyone, but she secretly admired her sister for having so much style.

Livvy was always trying to give her a make-over. One night last year when they were juniors, she allowed Livvy to work on her—lipstick, mascara, even streaks in her hair.

When she had finished, Livvy started to smile. "I don't think so," she said, holding her hand over her mouth. "I don't think so."

She turned the mirror to Destiny, and they both started to laugh. They collapsed to the floor, knocking over Livvy's makeup mirror, laughing until tears rolled down their cheeks.

Destiny thought about that night often. It was just a few weeks before their mother died, a few weeks before tragedy turned their lives upside down. And it was a night she felt so close to her sister, a night their closeness overcame their many differences.

Now Livvy tossed her cigarette down and stamped it out with the toe of her sandal. "You're already packed?" she asked Destiny.

Destiny nodded. "Well, yeah. Dad and Mikey will be here at the crack of dawn tomorrow. You should get started. Your stuff was spread all over your cabin."

Livvy grinned. "I know. I'm a slob." She and Cory exchanged glances.

"I'll help you, if you want," Destiny offered.

"Thanks. I'll do it later. We're all going to meet by the lake. Did someone tell you? The counselors and the J.C.s. We're going to stay up all night and get totally trashed."

Cory flashed Destiny a thumbs-up and a toothy grin. "Last chance to party."

Destiny sighed. "Well, can't you just pack up first?"

Livvy snapped at her. "I said later, *Mom*!" Her expression immediately softened. "Oh. Sorry."

But the word hung in the air between them.

And they shared the same thought: *We don't have a mom.*

Our mom killed herself last year.

Livvy squeezed Destiny's hand. "Sorry, Dee. I'll be there in a few minutes. Promise," she said. Then she tugged Cory toward the woods.

Destiny turned and made her way up the hill to the cabins. The sun had dipped behind the trees. Crickets began to chirp. Renz's circle of girls had dwindled to two admirers. He raised his eyes to Destiny as she passed, and waved at her.

Destiny waved back. She saw him watching her as she reached the main lodge at the top of the hill. He's been watching me all summer, she thought. But he's never invited me for one of his late-night walks by the lake. I had to hear about them from the other junior counselors.

And Livvy. Yes, Livvy fell under his spell too. And it's no secret he spent a lot of time with her.

Is Nakeisha right? Am I jealous?

Well, yes.

She saw a group of counselors building a fire in the campfire circle. Ronnie Herbert, a J.C. Destiny had hung out with—just a friend— came running up, a blue-and-white Camp Blue Moon T-shirt pulled down over his baggy khaki shorts. Ronnie took a scrap of paper from his shorts pocket. "Can I have your e-mail, Destiny? Can we keep in touch?"

"Of course," she said. "You know, Providence isn't *that* far from Dark Springs. We could meet sometime."

"Cool." Ronnie scribbled down her e-mail address. Then he hugged her. "This is so hard, saying good-bye to everybody." He turned and saw Nakeisha walking toward the campfire circle. "Hey, Keish, wait up!" He took off after her, waving his slip of paper in the air.

Destiny made her way past the campers' cabins, empty and forlorn looking, some of the doors hanging open, revealing the bare bunk beds with their flat, gray mattresses. At the end of the row, she pulled open the door to Iroquois, the cabin she had shared with her campers.

She spotted a red hair scrunchy on the floor, the only sign that six eight-year-old girls had once lived here. Destiny's bags were lined up neatly in front of her bunk.

She sighed. Should I go across to Arapaho and start to pack up Livvy's stuff? I know Livvy will wait till morning and keep Dad, Mikey, and me waiting.

She considered it for a second, then decided, *No way*. That's *her* problem. I really *am* starting to think like a mom.

It's my last night at Camp Blue Moon, my last night before I have to go back to the real world—and I'm going to have FUN.

Destiny changed into jeans and a camp sweatshirt. Then she hurried back outside to help build the fire, unaware of the horror that awaited her.

Chapter Two
A Romantic Walk

$\mathcal{B}$y eleven o'clock, the campfire had burned down to a pile of crackling red and purple embers. The beer had run out—a mountain of empty cans poked up over the rim of a metal trash can—and bottles of red wine were being passed around a circle of six or seven counselors.

Destiny joined a group of junior counselors who had their own circle around their own small fire and were singing the familiar camp songs they had been forced to sing all summer, but adding crude and extremely gross new lyrics. They laughed and hugged each other and sang under the full moon, their faces reflecting the dying firelight.

Several couples had wandered away from the big campfire to make their way through the trees to the lake. Destiny saw Livvy disappear into the woods again with Cory Field.

"Good night. I'm outta here. Gonna get my

beauty sleep." Nakeisha crushed a Coke can in her hand and tossed it onto the pile of cans in the trash. "Catch you in the morning, Dee. Don't leave without saying good-bye, okay?"

Destiny laughed. "We've already said good-bye twelve times!" She watched her friend climb the hill to the cabins.

I'm going to catch some sleep too, Destiny decided. I know Dad and Mikey will be here at six A.M. on the dot.

She waved good night to her friends, climbed to her feet, and began to walk to her cabin. She was halfway up the hill when a figure stepped out of the shadows and blocked her path.

"Renz. Hi," Destiny said, nearly walking into him.

"I've been looking for you," he said softly.

"Really? Me?" She could feel her cheeks growing hot. *Don't sound like such a jerk.*

His smile was dazzling, even in the darkness. She could feel his eyes burn into hers. "It's still early. You're not checking out, are you?"

"Well . . ."

He took her hand. "Want to take a walk? Down by the lake? We haven't had a chance to talk for a long time."

"Yes. Okay," she heard herself say.

Renz squeezed her hand. "Good," he whispered.

He slid his arm around Destiny's shoulders and guided her down the hill. He pointed at some counselors dancing around the dying fire. "Have you ever seen such bad dancing? It's a good thing it's dark and they can't really see each other."

Destiny frowned. "They've had too many beers to care."

He stared hard at her. "You don't like to drink?"

She shook her head. "One beer and I start giggling like a ten-year-old."

Why am I telling him this?

She followed him down the grassy hill to the narrow dirt path that led through the trees. "Isn't it a beautiful night?" He pulled her close as they walked. "But also a sad night. No one wants to go home."

"It was an awesome summer," she replied. "Livvy and I . . . we had a very bad year. Camp was the perfect escape."

Renz lowered his hand from her shoulders and slid it around her waist. "You want to escape from your home?"

He helped her over a fallen log. They followed the path past a row of low pine shrubs. "No. Of course not," she said. "I'm looking forward to going back. You know. Senior year and everything."

"It's so nice down here," he said softly, bringing his face close to hers. "The pine needles smell so fresh, and I love the way the lake glows under the moonlight. Let's pretend we're not going home tomorrow, Destiny. Let's pretend we're going to stay here in the woods forever."

She laughed.

Is he for real?

He led her to a broad tree stump near the water, and they sat down. The lake shimmered like silver under the light of the pale full moon. He wrapped his hands around hers and held them in her lap.

My hands are ice cold. Can he tell how nervous I am?

"The lake looks beautiful without a hundred screaming kids splashing around in it," she said.

He flashed her his dazzling smile. "I've been watching you all summer," he whispered.

She raised her eyes to his. "You have?"

"I hoped we would be able to spend time getting to know one another."

Destiny rolled her eyes. "It's the last night of camp, Renz. What makes me think I was the last girl on your list?"

He didn't answer. Instead, he placed a hand gently under her chin, brought her face to his, and kissed her.

A short kiss, but sweet.

Destiny blinked. "You're very nice," she said. "But I know you've brought every female counselor and J.C. down here this summer."

"They weren't like you," he whispered.

"Oh, right," she said.

"But I'm telling the truth," he insisted. "They weren't like you, Destiny. *Believe me. They weren't like you.*"

Chapter Three

"It Won't Hurt for Long"

Renz kissed her again, longer this time, holding his hands on the sides of her face. He saw her eyes close. He felt her body relax.

She's enjoying it. She's beginning to feel what I feel.

But when she finally pulled away, Destiny laughed. "You're much too old for me, Renz." She squinted at him. "How old are you, anyway? Nineteen? Twenty?"

He grinned. "I turned two hundred last month. You're right. Much too old for you."

"Well, I know one thing. You're not like the guys in my high school. Where did you grow up? In Italy?"

Renz nodded. *I don't want to talk. I didn't bring you down here to talk.*

"I grew up in the north, in the hills where there is poverty—and strangeness."

He squeezed her hands. The pale moonlight

sparkled in her blond hair.

"Strangeness? Like what?"

"The people in my village had many superstitions and many fears," he told her, speaking softly, holding her close. "They were most terrified of the ancient vampires who lived in the caves that circled our village. The vampires were said to fly out at night in the shapes of blackbirds and bats. They would attack the villagers—men, women, and children—and empty their veins of blood."

Destiny gave him a playful shove. "You're trying to scare me, right?"

Renz nodded. "Yes. Actually, I was born in Philadelphia."

She laughed at his joke.

Pulling her closer, Renz's skin tingled with excitement. His mouth, his throat—they suddenly felt so dry. . . . He felt alert. Alive. Ready.

He held her by her arms and lowered his face to hers. He whispered, "Do you believe in vampires, Laura?"

With a short gasp, Destiny jerked her head back. "Excuse me? Vampires? And who's Laura?"

He stared at her, licking his lips. His whole

body tingled. He knew his hands would tremble if he let go of her. "Laura? Well . . . you remind me of someone, that's all."

He pulled her close again. Her expression softened. "I've thought about you, too, this summer," she said, avoiding his eyes.

She's shy like Laura, he thought. Not like her twin.

"And did you notice me watching you?" he asked eagerly.

She hesitated. "Well . . ."

He kissed her again. Lightly. He was so afraid to move too fast. He had waited so long to bring her here, to bring her to this moment.

But now the moment was here.

"I'm so happy I found you again, Laura," he whispered, gazing into her eyes. "I've been searching for you for so many years. I knew I'd find you again."

Those words made her struggle to pull free. But he grasped her arms tightly and held her in front of him. "Don't pull away, Laura. Tonight we are reunited."

"Renz—what the hell are you talking about? Let go of me! Now you're really scaring me."

"Don't be scared, darling. I know you have

waited for this moment as I have. It won't hurt for long. I promise it won't hurt for long. And then we will be together once more, together forever."

She squirmed, struggled to swing her arms, to lash out at him with both fists. "Let go. Let go, you creep! Are you crazy?"

Staring into her eyes, he let her struggle. Staring deeply . . . penetrating her mind.

She uttered a long sigh and settled back, limp in his arms.

"That's better, Laura. You feel calm now. You don't want to resist me. Tonight under the full moon I shall drink your blood, and you shall drink mine. Two long drinks, that's all it will take, darling. And then you will be Laura again. Then you will be immortal like me. And we will live together forever."

Destiny made a weak attempt to squirm free.

"Shh," he whispered. "Don't try to move. Don't try to think, darling. Keep staring into my eyes. That's right. See? Your mind is emptying. You remember nothing. You are floating in a cloud."

Bleating sounds escaped her lips, like a tiny, frightened animal caught in a trap. Her head fell back, her throat pale in the moonlight.

Pale and soft. And delicious.

"I have fogged your mind, and you won't remember a word I've said. You won't even remember *me* until I want you to. Until I am ready to fly with you, to spend every night—for eternity—with you."

Renz leaned forward, lowering his face to her throat. "You feel nice, don't you, Laura? You feel dizzy and happy, and the stars are spinning so gracefully, aren't they? It's all so beautiful and soft, isn't it, darling? So romantic. You always were so romantic."

Her soft cries stopped. Destiny stared up at him open-mouthed, her eyes glassy, her chest moving rapidly up and down.

Renz gently pulled down the neck of her sweatshirt. His curved fangs made a wet *slick* sound as they slid down from his gums. He worked his tongue over the fangs, trying to wet them. But his mouth was dry as sand.

Finally, he could resist no longer. He lowered his head, pushed out his bristled tongue, and licked her neck. Licked it, his rough tongue scraping over the soft skin. Licked it hungrily.

Then he opened his mouth wide and with a

groan from deep in his gut, brought the fangs down. Pierced the pale skin. Sank the sharp fangs deep into her throat.

And began to drink.

Chapter Four

"What Does He Want With Me?"

Destiny gazed up at the purple night sky. White dots of light shimmered and danced. The full moon, surrounded by glimmering stars, grew brighter, brighter . . . until she had to lower her eyes.

She felt Renz's hot forehead against her chin. His thick black hair tickled her flesh. She heard a lapping sound, like water running. No. Like a dog drinking noisily from a bowl.

Destiny felt a gentle pain at her throat, softer than the bite of a mosquito. With a sigh, Renz raised his head.

What was that dark liquid spilling down his chin?

Destiny struggled to think. But the moon shone so brightly—like a harsh spotlight—and the stars danced so giddily, she felt dizzy, sleepy. She couldn't focus.

She liked Renz's smile, his wide eyes, his

forehead gleaming with jewels of sweat. But why were his teeth curling over his chin? And what was that dark liquid that smelled so sharp and metallic?

Focus. Focus.

She blinked hard. But it all seemed fuzzy, far away.

She gazed into Renz's eyes, glowing black, staring down at her. And as she stared, she realized to her amazement that she shared his thoughts.

She saw a young, black-haired boy, six or seven, bare chested, in ragged, stained trousers that came down just below his knees. The boy, dirty faced, ribs poking out, carried a fishing pole much too long for him. He dragged it along a dusty road.

Destiny knew it was Renz—Renz as a young boy. Renz in the northern Italian village where he grew up in poverty.

It's as if he is showing me his life, she realized. He's sharing his story with me.

She saw the boy return home slump-shouldered, tears running down his cheeks. No fish on the line. Destiny recoiled as she saw the grizzled, weary-looking man—Renz's father—give the boy a backhanded slap that sent him reeling into the wall.

Ouch. She could feel the slap, feel the pain spread over her cheek.

She tried to blink the pain away. And when she opened her eyes again, the boy was on a ship, ocean waves tossing against its gray sides. Frothy water washed over the swaying deck where the boy—young Renz—stood so uncertainly at the rail, frightened, one little face in a crowd of older, frightened faces.

Destiny could see the pictures clearly in her mind.

She saw the boy covering his tattered clothes with a heavy, gray overcoat that was much too big for him. Saw him arriving in New York City, then trudging through the streets, dodging horse-drawn carts and carriages, everyone dressed in black, the street a sea of black hats, all the men wearing hats.

How long ago this must have been.

She closed her eyes, and now the boy had grown into a young man. She recognized Renz—his proud way of standing, his loping walk, the black hair bouncing on his head as he strode down the street.

She watched as Renz suddenly turned into a narrow alley crammed with trash and stacks of old newspapers. And then she saw another man, lanky and pale, with straight white hair pulled back in a loose-flowing ponytail. The man had silver-gray eyes, a stubble of white beard. He wore a navy-blue suit and had a navy cape draped over one shoulder.

Destiny watched the two shake hands. She understood. Renz recognized the man from his ship, the ship that carried him to America. Yes, the man was from Renz's village.

Destiny cried out as the happy reunion suddenly turned violent.

The white-haired man pushed Renz against the building wall. Destiny watched the yellowed fangs curl down. Watched the man sink his teeth into Renz's throat and drink, blood running down the front of his dark suit.

Then Renz bit hard into the old man's neck and began to lap up his blood. They were drinking each other's blood! She couldn't bear to watch.

She closed her eyes, but the images continued to flood her mind. She saw Renz prowling the streets once again, but this time at night, only at night. She watched him attack birds and squirrels in the park, sink his teeth into their bellies, and drink.

And she felt his thirst, felt the overpowering need that forced him to seek out victims—human victims—and drink, drink until the thirst was momentarily quenched.

She saw him struggling to keep his secret. And then she felt his fear as he realized his secret had been uncovered. Men were collecting weapons, preparing to hunt him down. She felt his terror, and then she watched him flee.

She saw a blur of towns and villages cloaked by the dark of night. And she watched him settle far away from the city, far away from those who meant to destroy him. A small New England town where the winters were long and the days were short.

Another blink. She saw Renz in the moonlight with a beautiful young woman. The woman dressed in a simple blue gown, her blond hair flowing down the back of her dress.

She looks like me, Destiny realized. And at once, she knew the young woman's name: Laura. The high cheekbones, the green eyes, the fine blond hair . . . Laura resembles me so much.

Except for the sadness in her eyes.

Such sad eyes.

Destiny saw how much Renz loved Laura. He adored her. And then in another blink of her eyes, she saw Laura's open casket. The sad eyes shut forever. It happened so quickly.

She saw Renz's angry tears. And heard his angry, desperate vow to find Laura again. To be reunited with her no matter how many decades or centuries it took.

Destiny saw it all as the stars swirled above her and the sky continued to spin.

But I'm not Laura, she told herself, the world so distant now as if she saw it through a curtain of gauze.

I'm not Laura.

So what docs he want with me?

Chapter Five

"I'll Follow You Home"

Renz gazed down at her, breathing deeply, feeling the cool night air brush against his hot face. He licked his lips, the rich, iron-tasting liquid so sweet on his tongue.

The lake lapped gently against the grassy shore. Trees whispered and shook. Somewhere a night dove cooed. Renz felt alive again; alive and strong.

He felt happy, almost giddy. Reunited with his lost love.

He wanted to shout it into the wind. He wanted to fly over the lake, crying her name.

"Laura . . . Laura . . . !"

But first we must finish, he told himself. I have drunk deeply. And now it is her turn.

I'm here, darling. I know you have waited as long and impatiently as I have.

He had searched for Destiny at the last full moon. But to his dismay, she had left camp on a canoeing overnight. He had to wait four long weeks for the full moon to rise again.

And now finally, here she was in his arms, ready to take the final step.

"Oh." He raised his head abruptly, hearing the snap of a twig on the ground.

No. No. No.

He pulled himself up. Tilted Destiny's head up. Slid his arm around her shoulders.

He could smell someone approaching. A girl. He could hear the blood pumping through her veins before she even appeared.

He turned as Nakeisha stepped into view.

"Destiny? I was looking for you. I forgot—" Nakeisha saw Renz with his arm around Destiny. "Oh. Sorry. I didn't know. I mean . . . catch you later."

Nakeisha spun around and darted into the thicket of trees.

Had the spell been broken?

Renz turned back to his love, his prize.

Destiny sat up, shaking her head. "Wow. I feel so dizzy."

"Don't move," Renz whispered. "You're okay." He reached to hold her, but Destiny jumped up and stepped away from him. "Come back, Destiny. Just for a few moments."

She blinked at him. "No. Sorry. It's late. And I feel so . . . weird."

She waved to him, blinking in confusion. Then she took off, running through the tall wet grass, moonlight reflecting off her hair.

He watched until she vanished behind tall pines. Then he opened his mouth in a cry of fury.

So close. So close, my darling Laura. But you didn't finish.

His skin tingled. The hair on the back of his neck prickled. He could still taste her blood on his tongue.

We *will* be together for eternity, Laura.

I will follow you. I will follow you home.

You won't know me. You won't remember me. So it will be easy.

Our blood will mingle. I promise.

I will come. I will come for you.

I won't let you get away this time.

Part Two

Chapter Six

"Did She Stay Out of Trouble This Summer?"

Destiny watched her dad's SUV rumble up the hill toward the cabins. "Crack of dawn," she muttered, shivering in the damp morning air. I knew he'd be the first to arrive.

"Hey, Livvy!" She cupped her hands and shouted into Arapaho. "Wake up! Dad and Mikey are here."

"Give me a break. I'm packing," her sister shouted back.

Destiny yawned and hugged herself, wrapping the sleeves of her camp sweatshirt around her shoulders. Why am I so tired this morning?

I see Dad didn't get the front fender fixed. And the car is covered with dust. He probably didn't wash it all summer.

Destiny's mom had always taken care of the practical matters, allowing her husband to spend all his thoughts on his veterinary practice and his research.

With Mom gone, the car will just disappear under a mountain of dirt, Destiny thought. "Hey, Liv—do you need any help?"

No answer.

Destiny turned and saw Chris Harvey, the lanky, blond-haired arts-and-crafts counselor, bent over, throwing up noisily against the side of his cabin.

"Late night, Harvey?" someone shouted from one of the cabins.

"How about a beer, Harvey?"

Harvey was in no position to reply. Destiny watched him stumble into his cabin, wiping his face with his T-shirt.

Car doors slammed. She turned and saw Mikey come bursting from the car. Slipping in the dewy grass, she ran down to meet him.

"Hey, you're tall!" she said, wrapping him in a hug. She brushed her hands through his thick, coppery hair.

"Dad got me a new game," he said, holding up his Game Boy. "See? It's like a NASCAR race."

"I haven't seen you all summer, and you just want to show me a game?" She hugged him again.

"Yuck. Stop doing that." He pulled back.

"It's a really awesome game. I'll show you how to play on the way back." He glanced around. "Where's Livvy?"

"Packing. Go help her." She gave him a shove toward their sister's cabin.

He took off toward Arapaho. "Hey, Liv, we're here! Check out my new game!"

Destiny turned to see her dad come striding up the hill, arms outstretched, a smile on his face. His glasses glinted red in the early-morning sunlight. The thick tuft of gray hair bobbing on top of his head was unbrushed as usual. His heavy gray eyebrows moved up and down like two fat caterpillars above the glasses.

"I believe I know you from somewhere," he said.

Destiny hugged him hard. She pressed her cheek against his. "Ouch. You didn't shave."

He rubbed his chin. "Guess I forgot."

His beard has turned white, Destiny observed. And he looks so tired.

She squinted at him. "Have you been putting in more long nights in your lab?"

He nodded. "Pretty much." His smile was sad. "With everyone gone and the house empty, what else should I do?"

Destiny swallowed hard. "Well, we'll all be home now. It won't be so quiet anymore."

"That's what I'm afraid of!" he said. Behind the glasses, his pale blue eyes flashed.

They both laughed.

Livvy emerged from her cabin in shorts and a sleeveless T-shirt, dragging a suitcase, a backpack, and three other canvas bags, clothes spilling over the tops. "I couldn't fit it all in," she said.

She dropped everything and ran to hug her dad. "Hey, I missed you!"

He stepped back to study her. "You look positively healthy."

Livvy frowned. "Is that a compliment?"

He continued to stare. "No tattoos?"

"Of course not, Daddy. I promised, remember?"

He turned to Destiny. "Did she stay out of trouble this summer?"

"No way," Livvy said before Destiny could reply. "Why would I want to stay out of trouble?"

Dr. Weller chuckled. He raised his eyes to Livvy's cabin. "We're missing one family member. Where's Mikey?"

Livvy rolled her eyes. "He found some new

kind of worm he's never seen before under my bed. He was following it around the cabin, studying it. He's just like you, Dad, fascinated by animals and insects."

"Our cabins are a great place to study mutant insect life," Destiny said. "He could be in there for hours."

"Mikey is definitely growing up," Livvy said. "He used to *eat* the worms. Now he just follows them."

"Let's start packing up the car," Dr. Weller said, massaging the back of his neck. He sighed. "We've got a long drive home."

"Dad looks so much older," Livvy said. She whispered even though they were upstairs in their room.

"It's just because his whiskers turned white," Destiny said.

Livvy shook her head. "He looks really tired. He's kinda stooped over. And didn't you notice how he keeps sighing all the time? His whole face is different. It's like sunken or something."

Destiny peered down the stairs to make sure the door was closed. The twins shared a long, low room above the garage. It had been empty storage space when the Wellers moved in and the girls were little. But their father built walls, painted, set down carpet, and turned it into a big room with lots of privacy that they could share.

Destiny loved the room because it was like having her own apartment. When her friends came over, they always hung out there.

"I think Dad's been working too hard," Destiny said, stuffing dirty camp clothes into a white laundry bag. "He didn't take any vacation at all this summer."

Livvy, sprawled on her bed, watched Destiny unpack. "He's been strange ever since Mom died, like a zombie or something."

"We all miss Mom," Destiny said softly. "It's just weird being back in this house without her. I keep expecting her to come up here and help us unpack."

"Me too," Livvy whispered.

They both fell silent. Destiny checked the bottom of her suitcase. Empty. She had finished unpacking. Her sister's bags sat against the wall, untouched.

"And what is Mikey's problem?" Livvy asked. "He played that dumb Game Boy game all the way home and barely spoke to us."

Destiny shrugged. "I'm worried about him. I asked him how he liked his day camp, and he said it was totally boring. He said he didn't make any new friends because he didn't want to. And he didn't learn to dive because there was too much chlorine in the pool."

"Oh, wow," Livvy said, shaking her head. "Is it shrink time for Mikey?"

Destiny sighed. "You know how close he was to Mom. And he's only eight years old, the poor kid."

She crossed the room and dropped down on the edge of her sister's bed. "It isn't going to be easy, Liv. We're really going to have to help out a lot more here at home."

Livvy leaned back against the headboard of her bed, crossing her legs in front of her. "Tell me something I don't know. I already quit the cheerleading squad so I could be home with Mikey afternoons, didn't I?"

She sighed. "This is our senior year. It's supposed to be totally awesome. You know. Fun? Exciting?"

"We'll have fun," Destiny said, reaching out and squeezing her sister's arm. "Don't worry.

We can still have fun."

She turned when she heard heavy footsteps on the stairs. "Hey—who's there?" she called.

"It's me!" a deep voice boomed in a heavy foreign accent. "I've come to drink your blood!"

Chapter Seven
She Can't Stop Screaming

Destiny jumped up and ran to the stairwell. Peering down, she saw their friend Ari Stark halfway up the stairs. Ari, short and stocky, his serious face topped by curly black hair, wore baggy khaki cargo shorts and a T-shirt with a grinning mummy across the front.

"Hey, what's up?" he called. "Check this out." He held up a DVD. Destiny read the title: *Curse of the Vampire's Daughter*.

Livvy came over to greet Ari. She groaned when she saw the DVD. "I am *so* not in the mood for another one of your gross vampire movies."

"But it's Part Three," Ari protested. His gums showed when he smiled. "It's the best one. The special effects are awesome."

Livvy tossed back her hair. "I'm, like, sick of awesome effects. What's so great about awesome effects?"

Ari looked hurt. Horror movies were his life.

"We haven't seen you all summer," Destiny said, "and you just want to sit and stare at a movie?"

"Yeah," Ari replied. "Well, hey. How was camp? Did they show any movies?"

"We didn't have time for movies," Livvy told him. "We were too busy having sex every night."

Ari's cheeks turned red.

Destiny and Livvy shared a smile. *He believes us.*

"And what did *you* do all summer?" Livvy asked him. "You have a paper route or something?"

"Ha ha." Ari's face was still red. "I just hung out. You know. I helped my dad a little at the restaurant. It's been kinda scary here in town."

Destiny's eyes went wide. "Scary?"

Livvy's cell phone rang. She ran to her desk and picked it up. "Yeah. Hi. Where are you? *Our* front yard? Well, yeah. Come up. We haven't seen you in months." She clicked off the phone.

"Who was that?" Destiny asked.

"Everybody."

"I missed you so much." Ana-Li May wrapped her arms around Destiny. "I kept trying your cell for weeks, but you never answered."

"The camp was deep in the woods," Destiny said. "My phone was useless. I missed you too. . . . What's different about you?" She stepped back to study her friend.

Ana-Li was tiny and thin, like a delicate bird. For such a little girl, she had a surprisingly deep, womanly voice. She also had a warm, winning smile, and enough energy for five people.

She gave Destiny a playful shove. "There's nothing different about me. You just forgot what I look like. You know. Out of sight, out of mind."

"I tried to e-mail you," Destiny said, "but my laptop—"

"So how was camp? Meet any great guys?"

"Not really. I made some good friends, though."

"Too bad," Ana-Li said. She waved to Livvy across the room. "I struck out too. That physics workshop I went to at M.I.T.? Geek City."

"Let's talk later. Just you and me," Destiny said. "I love what you did with your hair. Wish I could have such perfectly straight black hair."

"That's so funny," Ana-Li said. "I always wanted to be a blond."

Destiny tugged her friend's hair. "Maybe we should trade."

They both laughed.

Destiny turned to say hi to her other friends. They were all talking at once, their voices ringing off the low ceilings of the room above the garage. They sprawled on the cream-colored carpet, sat on the long, cushiony couch that divided the room between Destiny's territory and her sister's half, and perched on the edges of the beds.

Destiny felt a wave of happiness sweep over her. The house had felt cold and gloomy last spring when her mother . . . when her mother killed herself. So many tears. So many long silences.

And after it had happened, their friends suddenly treated the twins differently. No one made jokes. Everyone acted tense and awkward. The girls felt kids were watching them whenever they walked down the hall at school.

We weren't us anymore. We were the girls whose mother committed suicide.

Eight weeks of working at Camp Blue Moon

had helped Destiny get away from all that. And now her friends' voices warmed her, made her feel safe and comfortable in her house again.

Standing by the door, Destiny gazed around the room at everyone.

On one end of the couch, Ari was talking with Courtney DeWitt, gesturing wildly with his hands, as usual, telling her about a horror convention his cousin had taken him to.

Courtney hadn't changed a bit over the summer, Destiny saw. She was still skinny but round-faced, with her straight brown hair pulled back in a high ponytail, the kind everyone had in fourth grade.

"I hate this round face," she once complained to Destiny. "Every time my dad calls me Babyface, I just want to slug him!" Now she kept tugging at a hole in the knee of her jeans as she listened to Ari.

Destiny turned to Ross Starr on the other end of the couch. Ross had shaved his blond hair short over the summer, and everyone had to comment on it.

"What did *you* do this summer?" Destiny called to him.

Ross lowered the Mountain Dew can he'd

been chugging from. He flashed Destiny his winning smile. "I was a lifeguard. What a blast. Check out this tan."

"A lifeguard? For real? Where?"

"Jersey shore. My aunt has a house there."

"Did you rescue anyone?" Ari asked.

Ross's eyes flashed. "Well, no. But I had to give mouth-to-mouth a few times."

Everyone laughed. Destiny studied Ross. She'd been thinking about him all summer. "You've been working out?"

He grinned and flexed his biceps. "Check out this new bod. I think I want to live forever!"

"Why?" Ari asked.

"Think of all the girls I could have!" Ross smiled.

Livvy slid next to Ross on the couch arm. "You're bad," she said. She tugged playfully on the tiny silver hoop in his ear. "Did you miss me this summer?"

Ross squinted at her. "Which one are you?"

More laughter.

Destiny groaned. Is Livvy going to come on to Ross now? Does she have to have *every* guy?

Livvy and Ross were laughing about something. Livvy had her arm loosely draped around his shoulder.

I can't believe she's doing this in front of Courtney, Destiny thought. Livvy knows that Courtney is crazy about Ross. And she knows I have a crush on him too.

Fletch Green sat on the floor at the other end of the couch, his long legs crossed in front of him. He was talking into a cell phone.

When Fletch turned off his phone, Destiny made her way over to him. "You and Ross had summer basketball practice?"

He scratched his wavy, carrot-colored hair. "Didn't you hear? Coach Bauer called off summer practice. He's still messed up about his wife."

"Oh. Right."

Coach Bauer's wife died suddenly near the end of the school year. Marjory Bauer wasn't that old, forty-eight or forty nine, like the coach.

Bauer took a leave from school. Destiny remembered the rumors about him. That he went berserk or something. That neighbors could hear him talking loudly to himself late at night. That he had lost all interest in coaching the team.

"So are you guys gonna be any good this

year?" Destiny asked.

Fletch shrugged. "Ross and I are the only seniors. We'll have to step it up."

"Any more Coke?" Bree Daniel called from across the room. Sitting on the floor across from Ari and Courtney, Bree waved her empty soda can in the air.

Destiny really couldn't stand Bree, with her screechy mouse voice and her piles of streaky blond hair that fell over her face, and her pierced eyebrows that always made Destiny cringe. Bree had recently become Livvy's best friend. Or, as Destiny put it, Livvy's Bad Influence. Bree was the one urging Livvy to get a tattoo. And Livvy had never smoked a cigarette until she started hanging out with Bree.

"There's a kind of bug that spits out juice that makes human skin dissolve," Ari was telling Courtney. "I saw a show about it on the Discovery Channel."

"Ari, get a life," Fletch said. His cell phone rang. He raised it to his ear.

"I'll go downstairs and bring up some more drinks," Destiny said, making her way to the stairs. "And I think we have some bags of nacho chips." She raised her eyes to Livvy, who was practically in Ross's lap. "Hey, Liv, where's Dad? Have you seen him?"

Livvy shrugged in reply. She didn't take her eyes off Ross.

Weird, Destiny thought. Dad usually likes to come up and hang out with my friends. She started down the stairs.

"Do you have any cookies or anything?" Bree called after her. "I'm really starving."

Destiny pushed open the door and stepped into the kitchen. It took her eyes a moment to adjust to the single, dim ceiling light over the kitchen table.

"Oh. Hi," she said when she realized her dad was sitting at the table. Across from him sat Coach Bauer, his face solemn, hands clasped on the table. Destiny saw a deck of cards in front of her dad, but they appeared untouched.

"Hi, Coach," Destiny said. "How are you?"

He nodded. "Not bad." The orange light glared off his bald head.

Destiny turned to her father. "It's kind of dark in here, isn't it?"

"It's okay," he answered softly. "My eyes have been bothering me. Too much time in the lab, I guess." He removed his glasses and rubbed his temples.

Destiny pulled open the fridge. "Don't you two want to come upstairs? You know. Say hi."

They looked at each other. "Maybe later," Dr. Weller said. He picked up the deck of cards, but he made no attempt to deal them out.

Destiny grabbed a couple of six-packs of soda and balanced two bags of tortilla chips on top of them. She stopped at the doorway and turned back to the two men. "Come on up if you want. I think we're going to watch one of Ari's disgusting movies."

Her dad gave her a short wave. "Have fun."

When Destiny returned, her friends were in a heated discussion. Ari paced in front of the others, talking animatedly. "There were two of them," he was saying. "I'm not making this up."

"Two what?" Destiny asked, tossing a soda to Bree.

"Two deer," Ari said. "In Millerton Woods."

Destiny turned and stared at him. "What are you talking about? There are *hundreds* of deer in those woods."

"You've been away. You don't know what's

going on here," Ari said. "The two deer were dead. Their blood was drained. For real. Totally drained."

Livvy rolled her eyes. "And how many horror movies did you watch this summer?"

"It's not a movie," Ari insisted. "It's for real. I saw it on the news."

"Ari gets all his news on the Sci-Fi Channel," Ross said.

Ari didn't laugh. "There were other animals too. Raccoons and some squirrels. They were dead and their veins were empty, totally dry."

"Cute little squirrels and raccoons? You are *so* making me sick," Livvy said, holding her stomach.

Fletch shook his head. "Courtney, you'd better hide your cats if Ari comes over!"

Courtney let out a gasp. "Yuck. Who would suck cat's blood?"

"Feeling thirsty, Ari?" Bree asked. "I hear a dog barking next door. Yum!"

"It's not a joke," Ari insisted. "I . . . I know what it is. It's vampires. There are vampires out there who are doing this."

Ross and Fletch exchanged skeptical glances. Bree choked on her soda.

"Remember in third grade when Ari thought Mr. Hubner was a werewolf?" Ross said. "And it turned out he just didn't shave that day?"

Grinning, Fletch climbed to his feet and put his arm around Ari's shoulder. "Didn't you write a paper for Mrs. Klein about real vampires in history—and she flunked your ass?"

"Mrs. Klein is very narrow-minded," Ari said, pushing Fletch away. "Maybe if you would tear yourself away from your PlayStation and watch the news once in a while—"

"I saw it on TV," Ana-Li interrupted. "There was a scientific explanation for the whole thing. They said it was a virus. Some kind of mutant virus that was killing the animals."

"How can you believe that crap?" Ari demanded. "Of *course* they're going to say it's a virus. They're not going to tell you the truth."

"I think a virus that dries up all your blood is a lot scarier than vampires," Destiny said. "I mean, anyone can catch a virus—right?"

Courtney shivered. "Can we stop talking about this?"

Destiny tossed a bag of chips at Ari. "Are we going to watch your movie or what? Come on. We don't want to think about deer-eating viruses. Put in the movie."

Everyone moved to the couch or the floor to watch the TV. Ari slid the DVD into the player. Destiny dimmed the lights.

"Ari likes these vampire films because they're like his home videos," she heard someone whisper.

"I'm buying him a Silly Straw for his birthday," Livvy whispered. She made loud slurping noises.

"Everybody shut up," Ari said, squeezing into the center of the couch between Courtney and Ross. "These Vampire's Daughter movies are the *best*." He turned to Courtney, the most squeamish one there. "If it gets too scary, just close your eyes."

"I'm shutting them right now," Courtney said. She shut her eyes and grabbed onto Ari's arm.

The movie started with dripping, blood-red credits and booming organ music. The opening scene showed a black-caped female vampire creeping across a sleeping teenage boy's darkened bedroom. The boy woke up—just in time to scream—as the vampire sank her fangs into his throat.

"Hey, I think I know that guy!" Ross shouted.

"I'd like to know *her*," Fletch chimed in. "Is she hot or what?"

"She's got a definite dental problem," Bree added.

"She probably went to your father!" Livvy joked.

Bree's dad was a dentist. When they were in fourth or fifth grade, he did the braces for just about every one of Destiny's friends.

Destiny usually enjoyed the kidding around during Ari's dreadful horror movies. But as the film started, she suddenly felt strange—a fluttery feeling that began in her stomach and rose up to tighten her throat.

She took a long drink of soda, but it didn't seem to help. Sitting on the floor, she pressed her back against the front of the couch. She watched three vampires transform from bats into human form. They forced open the window of a girl's house and slipped inside.

Destiny's chest tightened. A cold sweat made her hands clammy. She swallowed hard.

Am I coming down with something? Why do I feel so strange?

On the screen, a tall, thin vampire, who reminded her a little of Fletch, crept up behind a couch where a teenage girl was reading a magazine. He lowered his head, sank his fangs into the startled girl's neck—

—and Destiny began to scream.

She opened her mouth in a high, shrill wail from somewhere deep inside her. She saw her friends turn to face her. Saw their shocked expressions.

She heard Ari's shouts. "What's wrong? What's wrong with her?"

She saw Ana-Li drop down beside her and throw her arms around her. "Dee, it's okay."

But no. It wasn't okay.

It wasn't okay because she couldn't stop screaming.

Chapter Eight

"You Won't Get Away From Me"

Cloaked in darkness, Renz stood in the street, staring up at the Wellers' house. A black mist encircled him, hiding him from sight as he moved across the front lawn to the house.

A silver scooter lay on its side at the edge of the driveway. Two cars were parked next to each other in front of the garage.

Destiny, you and your sister have visitors, I see.

He could hear their voices, their laughter. He raised his eyes and saw light in the window of the room at the top of the garage. The mist swirled around him as he moved up the driveway to the back of the house. Now he could hear the heartbeats in that room, hear the pulsing of blood through veins.

He gazed up at the window and listened for one heartbeat. One special heartbeat.

Laura, I am here for you. Laura, I can feel

your heart quicken for me.

You know I'm out here. You know I have followed you.

Yes, we must wait. We have weeks until the next full moon.

That will seem like an eternity to me, darling. But at least I can be nearby while I wait.

I will be watching you. I promise to stay near you all the time. I won't let you out of my sight.

You won't get away from me. Not this time.

And as you begin to change, to gain your powers, you will be ready for me. Ready to start your immortal life at my side.

Can you hear my thoughts, Laura?

Can you sense that I'm here? Can you feel my nearness?

He stood so still now, like a dark statue inside the circling dense fog. Listening . . . listening . . .

And then he heard the shrill scream from the room above.

Destiny's scream.

A smile spread over his lips. "Yes . . . yes!"

Chapter Nine
Such a Powerful Craving

*H*ow long did she scream? Destiny had no idea. When she finally stopped, it was like waking from a dream. Ana-Li held her tightly. Livvy stood above Ana-Li, pale, her mouth open in shock and concern.

Destiny blinked, then gazed at her friends. Her throat ached and her heart throbbed in her chest.

"Are you okay? What was *that* about?" Livvy asked, smoothing back Destiny's hair.

Ana-Li stepped back. "You—you frightened us."

Destiny shook her head, clearing it. "Sorry."

Livvy helped Destiny onto the couch. "Should I call Dad? Do you need a doc or something?"

"No, I'm fine," Destiny said, swallowing, her mouth still dry.

Livvy let out a long sigh. "Jeez, Dee. You

really freaked me out."

Ari shook his head. "You never used to scare so easy. Next time I'll bring an Olsen twins movie."

"That's not funny," Livvy said sharply. She held onto Destiny's hand. "What frightened you, Dee?"

Destiny rubbed her head, still feeling dazed. Her friends' faces kept going in and out of focus. "I don't know. I . . . can't explain it, Liv. But I feel okay now. Really."

Ana-Li handed her a Coke. Destiny took a long sip. The others were all on their feet, staring at her.

"I guess we're not going to finish the movie," Ari said. "Anyone want to come to my place and watch it?"

There were no takers.

Bree glanced around uncomfortably. "Maybe we should go."

A short while later, Destiny saw her friends heading to the stairs. "Whoa, wait." She struggled to her feet. "It's early. Come on. You don't have to leave."

"Catch you tomorrow," Courtney said. "You should get some rest, Dee. You're just totally stressed, I guess." She and Bree, Fletch, and Ari disappeared down the stairs.

"Call me later, okay?" Ana-Li said with concern as she followed the others to the stairs.

Ross approached Destiny, rubbing his close-shaved head, his green eyes studying her. "Glad you're all right. That was kinda freaky."

Destiny forced a smile. "I was just trying to rescue us from that awful movie."

"You could be an actress in one of those vampire films. That was awesome screaming."

"Glad you liked it."

Why did I scream like that? Why?

Livvy quickly stepped between them. "You heading out?" she asked Ross. "I'll go with you."

He shrugged his broad shoulders. "Yeah. Sure."

"I'll help clean up later," Livvy said.

Destiny stood in front of the couch, surveying the clutter of paper cups, empty soda cans, tortilla chip bags. She listened to Ross and Livvy clump down the stairs. The back door slammed.

I told her this summer I had a major crush on Ross. How could she do this to me? A burst of anger burned her chest. It slowly faded as she continued to think about Livvy. She had worried about Livvy all summer.

No. Actually, she started worrying before the summer began. She wondered why her sister suddenly started hanging out with Bree Daniel. Bree was wild and kind of slutty and didn't care about school or much of anything else except partying. Bree's parents had divorced last year, and it turned out neither of them wanted custody of her. She went back and forth from one parent to the other, but she was pretty much on her own.

Why did Livvy want to copy her?

And why did Livvy go after *every* guy in camp this summer? What was she trying to prove?

Destiny spent so many nights lying on her cot in the small camp cabin after lights out, staring up at the shadowy ceiling, worrying about her twin.

Mom didn't love us enough to stay with us. Is that why Livvy is so desperate to find love everywhere else?

Whoa. *You're* the one who freaked out tonight, Dee. You'd better not try to be Livvy's shrink.

With a sigh, she started to collect the trash.

This is so typical. Livvy runs out and leaves me here to clean up.

She carried the litter down to the kitchen. "Dad—hi."

He hadn't moved from the kitchen table. Alone now, bathed in the dim, orange light from above, he had a veterinary journal spread out in front of him. He stood, pushing his glasses up on his nose.

"Poor Coach. I don't know how to cheer the man up," he said, moving to the sink and rinsing out a mug.

"You both looked pretty grim to me," Destiny said. She leaned her head against his shoulder. "You okay, Daddy?"

"Define *okay*."

She gave him a shove. "*You* define it."

He shrugged. "I'm enjoying my work a little."

"Yeah?"

"Well, taking care of the puppies with diarrhea and cockatoos with seeds stuck in their beaks isn't too exciting. But my research work is keeping me on my toes."

He looks so much older up close, Destiny thought. I've only been away a couple of months. His skin didn't used to look so drawn and powdery. And his eyes used to be bright and alive. All the color seems to have faded away.

"What are you doing in the lab?"

"It's hard to explain. It's a kind of stem-cell research. Only with animal tissue. You know, animals get a lot of illnesses that could be genetic. If I can alter the genetic makeup, maybe I can eradicate some of the illnesses."

"Sounds like a lot of laughs, Dad. And what do you do for fun?"

"I stand here and let you make fun of me."

They both laughed. He hugged her. "I'm glad to have you girls back. It was awfully quiet around here all summer. And it was nice to have your friends in the house tonight. Great to hear all that laughing and screaming."

Mainly screaming, Destiny thought.

She said good night and hurried back upstairs to her room.

Hours later, Destiny awoke bathed in sweat, silvery-cold moonlight washing over her from the open window. She sat up in bed, feeling shaky, her skin tingling.

What time is it? She squinted at the clock

radio on the nightstand beside her. One forty-five?

Mopping her forehead with her nightshirt sleeve, Destiny sat up, wide awake now. And thirsty. She kicked off the covers and stood up.

I'm wide awake. And I need to do something about this thirst.

No. It was more than thirst. Her stomach growled. Hungry . . .

Starving.

I feel empty, completely empty. I have such a powerful craving.

Craving . . . for what?

In the rectangle of moonlight, she pulled on a pair of jeans and a T-shirt. Then she crept barefoot to the stairway. Down the stairs, so lightly the floorboards didn't squeak once. To the kitchen door and out into the cool, clear night.

Crickets chirped loudly—pounding in her ears—as if the volume had been cranked up. All of her senses alive and alert now.

Heart pounding, Destiny followed her hunger—around the side of the house, past the garden hose left tangled on the ground, past a clump of tall weeds, past Mikey's silver scooter beside the driveway.

Such a strange, powerful craving. Her mouth watering now. The back of her neck prickly and cold.

She began to jog, bare feet slapping the dew-wet grass.

She stopped when she saw the rabbit hunched at the side of the driveway. Its ears perked up. It stiffened, then froze in place.

Destiny dropped to her hands and knees in the grass.

She swallowed hard. She tried to force down her hunger. But her whole body ached with it.

Slowly, slowly, she began crawling over the grass.

I'm hunting . . . hunting like an animal.

Why am I doing this? I *love* little bunnies. I want to learn to take care of little bunnies—like Dad.

I love them. Yes, I love them.

Love them.

Love them.

She pounced.

The rabbit let out a weak squeal as Destiny grabbed it around its middle. As she tightened her hands around it, she could feel its heart thudding, feel its warmth in her cold hands, feel its chest heaving up and down.

I love bunnies.

I love bunnies.

I'm so hungry.

She stretched the rabbit out, baring the pink skin of its belly. She raised the soft belly to her mouth—

—and *someone else's hands* grabbed at the head. *Someone else's hands* tugged the rabbit away from her.

"NO!" Destiny whispered. She pulled the wheezing rabbit back with a hard, desperate tug—and raised her eyes. . . .

"Livvy—no!"

"Give . . . it . . . back." Livvy grabbed its ears and pulled.

The rabbit let out a final squeal.

Destiny had it by the middle. She lowered her head and sank her teeth into the soft, warm flesh.

The rabbit jerked, then went limp.

And both girls buried their faces in the warm body, and fed . . . fed so hungrily on the warm blood . . . satisfied the craving, the new craving, their frightening new hunger.

Destiny heard a rustling in the trees.

Was someone there?

She didn't care. She had to drink. She couldn't stop.

Finally, the rabbit corpse lay like a crumpled bag in their hands. Destiny heaved it into the hedges. She felt the thick, warm blood rolling down her cheeks, her chin.

Still on all fours, she stared at her sister. Panting hard. The sweet metallic taste on her tongue, on her lips.

Like an animal, she thought. Like a wild beast.

A hoarse groan escaped from Destiny's lips. And then finally, she found her voice. "Livvy," she whispered. "Livvy, what has happened to us?"

Part Three

Chapter Ten

"We'll Get Back to Normal"

A short while later, Destiny and Livvy were in the long T-shirts they slept in, standing awkwardly across from each other in their room. Destiny had turned on all the lights—the lamps, the ceiling lights, even the desk lamp—frightened that the darkness might swallow them up or turn them into creatures again.

"I . . . don't know what to say," she whispered.

"Oh, Destiny!" Livvy cried, and flung her arms around her sister. She pressed her face against Destiny's cheek and let her tears fall with her sister's.

"I'm so scared," Livvy said, when they finally let go of each other. "That was so . . . horrible."

Destiny pulled Livvy over to her bed. They sat down together. Livvy clasped her hands tightly in her lap. Destiny kept rubbing her face. She had taken a long, hot shower. Had she washed all the blood away?

"I'm not sure what happened out there," she said. "I just suddenly felt so hungry."

"Me too," Livvy whispered. "It was like . . . I couldn't help myself. I couldn't stop myself."

Destiny nodded. She bit her lip to keep more tears from coming.

"We killed that little rabbit," Livvy said, tugging at her long, wet hair. "We ripped it apart, Dee, and we—we drank . . ." Her voice faded.

Destiny didn't reply. She stared hard at a spot on her sister's neck. "Let me see that." She scooted closer and brushed a tangle of Livvy's hair out of the way.

"Dee, what is it?"

"A little red mark." Destiny rubbed her finger over it. "A tiny scab."

"Oh my God!" Livvy whispered. "Dee, you've got one too."

Destiny uttered a soft cry. They stared at each other, the two sisters suddenly so close, yet each lost in their own horrifying thoughts.

Tiny throat wounds . . . the overwhelming urge to feed on animal blood . . . Ari's story about vampires loose in the woods . . . animals drained of their blood . . .

The terrifying word—*vampire*—hung silently between them. Destiny refused to say it.

"It's the virus," Destiny said, breaking the silence. She coiled her hair around her finger, tangling it and untangling it. "That's it."

"Virus? What are you talking about? You mean the virus Ana-Li was talking about?"

Destiny nodded. "We caught it."

"I guess that's possible," Livvy said, shaking her head. "But I don't feel sick. Do you?"

"No," Destiny whispered. "But these marks on our necks . . . maybe we should talk to Ari," she said, thinking out loud. "We could swear him to secrecy, and—"

"Are you crazy?" Livvy jumped to her feet. "We can't tell *anyone* what we did. It's so . . . sick. It has to be a secret. We can't let anyone know."

"But Ari knows about these things," Destiny argued. "You heard him tonight, talking about the deer in the woods. He's a total expert on everything strange happening in the world."

"Dee, Ari lives in a total fantasy world. He spends all his time at the movies and on *Star Trek* websites. He is a sci-fi geek. He thinks half the teachers in school are werewolves and zombies!"

"Okay, okay." Destiny motioned for Livvy to lower her voice. "Sit down. I'm just saying he knows a lot of stuff. I don't know who else could help us—do you?"

"Well . . ." Livvy lowered her head, thinking. "Maybe Dr. Curtis? If it *is* a virus, he would—"

"No way," Destiny interrupted. "We can't go to our family doctor. He'd tell Dad."

"Oh. You're right."

"And we can't tell Dad," Destiny whispered, glancing to the stairs. "We can't let him and Mikey know. Dad is still messed up over Mom. It's been six months, and he's not getting any better. He seems really depressed. It scares me. He doesn't need any more bad news. I think it would just put him over the edge. And Mikey . . ."

"Mikey has changed too," Livvy said. "He never used to be so skittish. This afternoon, a cat wandered into the yard, and Mikey ran into the house. He never was afraid of cats or dogs. It was sad to see him run away like that."

"He never used to spend so much time in his room," Destiny said. "Mikey is definitely very troubled. We have to be careful, Liv. We can't let Mikey know about us. We don't want to scare him."

"Scare *him*?" Livvy whispered. "*I'm* scared, Dee. I'm really, really scared." Her body seemed to crumple, her shoulders shook, and she began to sob.

Destiny wrapped her in a tight hug. "We'll get back to normal, Liv," she whispered. "We won't let it happen again. We'll find a way. I know we will."

But a terrifying thought lingered in her mind:

What if we don't?

What if we don't?

Chapter Eleven
Ari's Frightening News

As the morning sun began to rise, Destiny turned away from the light. *My eyes, they're burning. My eyelids feel like they're on fire! Did the sun always shine so harshly into the room?*

"Livvy, are you awake?" Destiny called in a low whisper. "Do you feel the sunlight? Do your eyes hurt?"

"Yes. What's with the light? Ow."

"I don't know." Destiny hurried to the window and shut the blinds. She squinted at the clock radio: six forty-five. "We have to hurry outside, Liv. Before Dad and Mikey wake up."

"Huh? What for?"

"The rabbit. I tossed it somewhere in the front yard. We have to find it and hide it where they won't find it."

Livvy scrambled to her feet, pushing the long tangles of hair off her face. Her nightshirt clung to her body, wet with sweat. "What a horrible night."

"Shhh. Just get dressed," Destiny ordered. "We'll hide the rabbit, then get back into bed."

They pulled on shorts and T-shirts, then tip-toed barefoot down the stairs and through the house to the front door.

Careful not to make a sound, Destiny pulled open the front door. The morning air smelled fresh and sweet.

Livvy stepped out first and Destiny followed, squinting up at the bright orange sun rising over the trees. "Ow. The sun is so bright."

Shielding their eyes, they crossed to the side of the yard and began to search along the hedge. "There it is." Destiny saw it first—the dead rabbit, curled like a limp glove on the grass.

She glanced around frantically. "Let's take it to the woods behind the backyard. No one ever goes there."

They made their way across the lawn to the hedge. The rabbit's eyes had sunken into its head. Its belly was ripped open. Dark, dried blood caked the gray fur.

"We did this," Livvy murmured.

Destiny felt her stomach tighten into a knot. "Don't talk. Let's just get rid of it." She took a deep breath. Then she bent down, swatted away a swarm of flies, and picked up the dead rabbit. "It's stiff."

Destiny turned and, holding the rabbit corpse in both hands, started to the back of the house.

"Good morning," a voice called.

Destiny looked up to see her dad jogging toward them, perspiration drenching the front of his gray sweatshirt. She whipped the rabbit behind her back.

"I had a nice run this morning," he said, mopping his forehead with his hand. "Hey, you two are up awfully early."

"Uh . . . I guess we got used to camp time," Destiny said.

"Yeah. Up at the crack of dawn," Livvy added.

"It'll take a while to get back to our old lazy routine," Destiny said. "You know. Staying out till two, sleeping till noon."

He continued to squint at them. "Maybe you should come running with me in the morning. It really gives me energy for the whole day."

"Maybe," Destiny said, gripping the rabbit corpse behind her.

"Hey, can you help me?" a voice called from the house.

They all turned to see Mikey, in his blue-and-white striped pajamas, standing at the front door. "Eddy escaped again," he shouted.

As Mikey ran across the lawn, Destiny let the rabbit fall to the grass behind her.

"That dumb hamster?" Livvy said. "How does he get out of his cage?"

Mikey shrugged. "I don't know. I was playing with him last night. Maybe I left the door open. I— hey, what's that?" Mikey pushed Destiny out of the way and stared down at the dead rabbit. "Oh, gross. What happened to it?"

Destiny spun around and pretended to be surprised. "Oh, my—what is it? A rabbit?"

"Looks like someone ran it over or something," Livvy said.

Their dad strode over and squatted beside Mikey. He scratched his graying hair as he studied the rabbit corpse. Then he grabbed it and turned it onto its back. "Nasty," he said. "Very nasty."

Destiny gazed at her father's face. *Does he suspect what really happened?*

Dr. Weller turned the rabbit over again.

"Maybe a fox did this. Hmmmm. Or maybe it's that virus everyone is talking about."

Destiny bent down, pretending to be concerned. "Virus?"

Her dad nodded.

Mikey gave Dr. Weller a shove that almost toppled him over. "The stupid rabbit's dead. What about Eddy?"

"Oh. Eddy." Dr. Weller jumped to his feet. "Come on. Let's go find the escaped convict!" He and Mikey went running into the house.

Destiny turned to Livvy. "Dad believes in that virus, but we know how the rabbit died. I . . . I'm so confused. I don't know what to think. We've got to talk to someone. You know. Find out more about what's been going on around here."

Livvy crossed her arms in front of her. "There's no way we're going to tell Ari what we did."

"Of course not," Destiny said. "But he knows so much about what's been happening in Dark Springs. Maybe he could help us. Maybe—"

"I promised Bree I'd hang out with her today," Livvy said. "Besides, I feel perfectly fine this morning. I think it was a virus, and now

I'm almost back to normal."

Destiny sighed. "Well, I don't feel normal. Every time I think about that rabbit—"

"Okay, okay. *You* go see Ari. He has a big crush on you anyway. So go talk to him. And listen to all his crazy ideas. But don't tell him anything about us, Dee. Don't even hint. You know what a total gossip he is. If you tell him anything, the whole school will know!"

Destiny stared at her twin. "Don't worry. We'll keep our secret—no matter what."

Ari's house was a ten-minute drive from Destiny's. She took the old banged-up Honda Civic Dad had driven to near-death, then passed down for the girls to share.

Ari lived in a long, rambling ranch-style house in the better section of Dark Springs. The street was blanketed in shade from the towering trees that lined both sides. Destiny pulled up the asphalt drive, passing two gardeners who were clipping the hedge that ran across the front of the yard.

She found Ari in his cluttered bedroom at the end of the long, carpeted hall. The walls were covered with framed horror movie posters.

DRACULA RISES ONCE AGAIN! proclaimed the poster over Ari's bed. Mounted on the wall above the poster, a fur-covered werewolf mask stared down at her.

Ari's bookshelves were jammed with books and magazines. A six-foot-tall plastic *Star Wars* Jedi Knight stood beside the bookcase, light saber raised, as if protecting them. The new Anne Rice novel lay facedown on Ari's unmade bed.

Ari had his back to her. He was hunched over his keyboard, clicking furiously, headphones over his ears. Destiny crossed the room and tapped him on the shoulder.

"Hey!" He jumped up, jerking the headphones off. "Destiny—whoa! You scared me."

"Sorry. You couldn't hear me." She raised her eyes to the monitor. "What's up?"

He set the headphones down on the desk and minimized the window he had been viewing. "Nothing really. These *Star Trek* chat rooms . . . they're so boring. I think it's all horny twelve-year-olds looking to hook up. No one wants to talk about anything serious."

Ari glanced back at his computer monitor. "It's strange. I'm still into *Babylon 5*, but no one else is anymore. It's like no one is loyal to anything. They're all into Yu-Gi-Oh and all this stuff that's for babies."

"It's tragic," Destiny said, trying to keep a straight face. But she couldn't. She burst out laughing.

Ari laughed too. "Okay, say it. I'm weird. Everyone thinks I'm weird. Whatever."

"I don't think you're weird, Ari." Destiny dropped down on the edge of the bed and picked up the Anne Rice book. "I think it's cool that you're into . . . stuff."

He looked at her. "You do?"

She nodded and gazed at the spread-winged bat on the book cover. The image sent a chill down the back of her neck.

"Well, what's up with you, Dee? What was that about last night? You totally freaked."

She shrugged. "I don't know. I think you scared me, Ari. You know. Talking about those deer in the woods and everything."

"Everyone was making jokes." Ari wheeled his desk chair up to her and sat down on it backward, resting his arms on the chair back. "But it isn't funny. It's for real."

"What's for real?"

"The dead animals in the woods with their blood drained. That's not any kind of virus." He shook his head. "Virus . . . that's what they put in the newspaper so people won't get scared. But I know I'm right. I know it has to be vampires."

"But, Ari—"

"And here's why I know I'm right. Do you know the latest? Know what I heard? I heard there are vampire hunters in Dark Springs."

"Vampire hunters? Ari, what are you talking about? That is *so* not possible."

"I read it online from two different people."

Destiny set the book down and clasped her hands in her lap. "You mean hunters like on *Buffy*?"

"Real vampire hunters, Dee. I heard they were training, getting ready."

"What does that mean? Getting ready for what?"

"It's a no-brainer. It means I'm not the only one who thinks there are vampires in Dark Springs. The hunters believe it too. And they are going to go after them and kill them all."

Chapter Twelve
"There's No Cure"

Destiny stared at Ari, thinking hard. She realized he was waiting for her to react, but she didn't know what to say. The silence hung heavily between them.

"One of the hunters was sitting in your kitchen last night," Ari said finally.

"Excuse me? You mean Coach Bauer?"

Ari nodded. "It's just a rumor," he said, lowering his voice.

The housekeeper entered the room, carrying laundered towels to Ari's bathroom. He waited for her to leave.

"I mean, I don't know it for sure. But some people in a chat room said Bauer had joined the hunters. One guy said Bauer was the leader, but I think that's crap."

Destiny swallowed. She pictured the coach and her dad sitting at the kitchen table so glumly, barely speaking, the light so low. "Coach

Bauer? A vampire hunter? It sounds crazy."

Ari shrugged. "Not that crazy. People talk about him. How he got weird after his wife died last spring. You remember. He had to take a leave from school."

"Give him a break," Destiny said. "The poor man's wife died. So he needed time off for a while. Ari, this kind of gossip is just ugly. My dad hasn't been the same since my mom died. Do you want to start rumors about him too? I don't think you can blame Coach Bauer for being upset."

"But the whole thing was strange. My family and I went to the funeral. It was a closed-casket funeral. My mom said that was very odd. Mrs. Bauer died of a heart attack. So why wasn't the casket open?"

Destiny shook her head. "I'm sorry. This is too dumb. Maybe it's a family tradition to keep the caskets closed. There could be a hundred reasons, Ari."

"But there's more," Ari insisted. "People said that after his wife died, they saw Bauer trapping rabbits and squirrels behind his house. He set out these traps all over his backyard, and he caught animals in them."

Destiny squinted at him. "For what? Why would he do that?"

Ari shrugged again. "Beats me. I'm just telling you what I heard. Maybe he was going to use the animals to lure and trap vampires. I don't know."

"That's crazy," Destiny insisted. "The whole thing is ridiculous."

"But cool," Ari said, grinning. "I mean, wouldn't that be *amazing* to see a real vampire? I'd join the hunters. Really. If they would take me, I'd join. I'd do anything to see a real, live vampire—wouldn't you?"

"No way. I think it would be terrifying." Destiny shuddered. She stared hard at Ari. "You really would join them?"

He nodded.

"It's totally outrageous," she said. "We live in a tiny, quiet town. How would someone in Dark Springs ever become a vampire?"

"It's easy, Dee. It could happen to anyone, I guess. Even people in Dark Springs. You just have to be bitten by a vampire."

"That's it? What happens after you're bitten? You become a vampire? That's all there is to it?"

He scratched his head. "Well, some of the books I've read say there's a little bit more. There has to be a full moon at its peak in the sky. And a vampire has to drink your blood under the light of the moon, and you have to drink the vampire's blood."

Destiny scrunched up her face. "Yuck. All that blood drinking is so gross." She suddenly realized she had her hand on the mark on her throat.

"I'm just telling you what I've read," Ari said.

"Well, is there a cure?" Destiny blurted out. "I mean, people who are bitten. Can they be cured?"

Ari thought for a moment. "I don't think so."

"You can't ever become normal again?" Destiny realized her voice had risen several octaves.

"No. There's no cure. I've never read about a cure. Maybe if the person is only a neophyte . . ."

"A what? A neophyte?"

Ari climbed to his feet. "I could give you some books to read, Dee, if you're interested." He started to his bookshelves.

"No. Just tell me what a neophyte is," she insisted.

"It's kinda like being a half-vampire. If a

vampire drinks your blood, but you don't drink theirs, you're only a neophyte."

"And—?"

"You'll be a neophyte until the next full moon. Then the vampire can finish you—exchange blood with you—and make the transformation complete."

Destiny could feel her heart pounding. "And what if he doesn't finish you? What happens to you?"

"You go crazy or something. Some books say you become like an undead creature, half-human, half-vampire. You spend all your time trying to satisfy your hunger for blood."

This is crazy, Destiny thought. This can't have anything to do with Livvy and me.

But the memory of last night—of the powerful craving, of hungrily devouring the rabbit's blood—made her tremble. Her mind spun with ugly, terrifying thoughts.

Destiny realized she had shut her eyes. She opened them to find Ari staring hard at her. "What's wrong, Dee?" he asked, his eyes penetrating hers as if searching for answers in them. "What's up with you? How come you're suddenly interested in vampires?"

She took a deep breath.

Ari dropped back into his chair and brought his face close to hers. "What's up, Dee? Come on. Tell me."

"Oh. Wow. Sorry," Destiny said, smoothing back her short hair. "I just remembered something. I promised Dad I'd go to the supermarket. And what am I doing? I'm sitting here listening to your disturbing vampire stories."

She started for the door. He remained sitting backward on his desk chair. "Hey, it's great that you came over, Dee. Glad you don't think I'm weird because I'm interested in vampires and stuff."

"It was interesting. Really."

He jumped to his feet. "Where are you going? The Stop and Shop on Sweetwater?"

"Well, yeah."

"I'll go with you. Mom and Dad are at the club, playing seventy-two holes or something. There's nothing in the house to eat."

Destiny had her shopping list in one hand and pushed the cart with the other. Ari tagged along beside her, muttering about how he couldn't decide what to buy.

"My dad is really losing it," Destiny said, shaking her head. "There's no food in the house. I don't think he's gone shopping in a month! His mind, it's just . . ." Her voice trailed off.

It was a little after two in the afternoon, and the long supermarket aisles were nearly empty. In the vegetable section, a white-uniformed boy was spraying water on the lettuces. In the middle of one aisle, Destiny saw an old woman, leaning heavily on the handle of her shopping cart, reaching for a box of cereal on a shelf high above her head.

"Where *is* everyone?" Ari asked. "It's so deserted. Do you think an alien invasion has taken place, and you and I are the last few people on earth?"

"That explanation wouldn't be first on my list," Destiny said.

"Did you see that *Twilight Zone* where a man wishes everyone would go away—and they do? That was a classic."

He continued to talk, but his voice faded from Destiny's mind. Instead, she heard a loud rush, like the roar of the ocean. She covered her ears, but she couldn't shut out the sound.

Blinking hard, she could see Ari talking, but

she couldn't hear him over the deafening roar. She stopped in front of the meat counter. Her mouth began to water. She swallowed hard.

The roaring sound faded as her hunger rose.

I'm not imagining this. I'm *so hungry*.

Supermarket music jangled in her ears. Her senses were suddenly alive. The tangy-sour aroma of the meat in the refrigerated shelves filled her nostrils.

Hungry . . .

Ari stood beside her, one hand on the side of her cart. She could hear the tinny supermarket music and she could hear the steady pulsing of the blood through her veins.

Her heart raced as the craving swept over her.

Ari was bobbing his head in time to the music. His pale throat suddenly gleamed in Destiny's eyes.

Her stomach growled with a gnawing emptiness. She could feel saliva dripping down her chin.

I can't help it. I can't stop it.

She grabbed Ari by the shoulder and lowered her mouth to his throat.

Chapter Thirteen
"I Need To Feed"

"*O*uch!" Ari gave a startled cry and pulled away. "Hey, supermarkets turn you on?"

Destiny wiped her chin. Her eyes stayed on his neck. She could see the blue vein pulsing down from his jawline.

"Dee, I didn't think you *liked* me." He leaned forward and kissed her. He glanced around to see if anyone was watching. Then he lowered his head to kiss her again.

I'm so hungry. I need to feed.

Yes. Yes. She wrapped her hands around his shoulders, preparing to pull him close and sink her teeth into his throat.

But no.

I can't. I can't do it to Ari.

It took all her strength to push him away.

He grinned at her, excited by her kisses.

He doesn't understand. I'm so hungry, I'd do anything . . .

"Ari, would you do me a favor?" Her voice came out tight, shrill through her clenched teeth. "My dad needs pipe tobacco. It's called Old Farmer, I think. Could you find it for me?"

He nodded, his eyes still wide. "No problem."

She watched Ari take off down the long aisle. When he was out of sight, she turned to the meat display. Her chest heaved and she began to pant. Her hands shook as she reached down for a package of meat.

A package of liver. A wet-looking slab of purple meat, dripping with blood.

Dripping . . .

Oh yes. Oh yes.

She lifted it off the shelf and brought it close to her face. The rich aroma of the meat, of the red blood, made her dizzy.

Oh yes.

With a loud grunt, she ripped away the shrink-wrapping. Then she raised the package to her face and began to drink. She sucked up the blood noisily, her tongue lapping the bottom of the package. Then she grabbed the slippery liver in one hand, held it over her head, and squeezed it, squeezed all the good juice from it, squeezed it into her mouth. Every drop. Every last drop.

It tastes so rich, so delicious. So . . . satisfying.

She shoved the slippery red meat into her mouth and chewed. She could feel blood running down her chin.

Lowering her eyes, she saw Ari returning, jogging up the aisle. "Oh, no." She pulled the raw liver from her mouth. A frantic moment. Where to hide it?

She opened her bag. Stuffed the liver into it and shut it.

Heart thudding, still dizzy with pleasure, Destiny wiped the blood off her chin with the back of her hand. She turned to greet Ari—but her eyes stopped at the nearest aisle.

A white-uniformed store clerk came running toward her, eyes wide, motioning to her, shouting, "Miss! Miss!"

He saw me. He watched the whole thing.

He saw me.

Chapter Fourteen
A Snack at the Pool

"Marco!"

". . . Polo!"

"Marco!"

". . . Polo!"

Destiny watched the group of kids playing in the shallow end of the pool. Two boys were having a splashing war. Water tossed up over her sneakers. The lifeguard, a tall, skinny guy with a fabulous tan, blew his whistle and pointed at them.

Destiny pushed her sunglasses up on her nose. The afternoon sun beamed brightly down from a clear blue sky. Eyes burning, she searched the crowded pool for her sister.

Some guys from school were hanging out near the volleyball net. She saw Ana-Li, racket in hand, heading to the tennis courts with a girl Destiny didn't recognize.

And who was that good-looking guy with

the wavy black hair standing in the shade by the fence? Despite the bright sun, he wore a black, long-sleeved shirt and black shorts.

Why is he smiling at me?

Do I *know* him?

"Hey, Dee—where's your bathing suit?" Courtney called from the snack stand. She and Bree had on string bikinis. They both held ice cream pops and waved them at Destiny.

Destiny hurried over to them, nearly colliding with two little girls running with pool floats toward the lawn chairs at the side.

"Gotta soak up these last rays," Bree said. "The pool closes on Friday."

"Boo hoo. I hate it when summer ends," Courtney said. "I can't believe I'm already thinking about what to wear the first day of school."

"I'm wearing this!" Bree declared, motioning to her bikini. "How about you, Dee?"

"Have you seen Livvy?" Destiny asked breathlessly, ignoring her question. "She left me a note at home. Said she was coming here."

Bree licked her ice cream. "She's right over there." She pointed. "She brought Mikey and his friend. See?"

Destiny saw Livvy in the pool. She turned and took off running, her sneakers thudding on the wet concrete.

"Hey, is anything wrong?" Courtney called after her.

Livvy saw Destiny and waved. She was pushing Mikey and his friend on a small, red plastic raft. "Where is your bathing suit?" Livvy shouted.

"I didn't come to swim. I . . . need to talk to you," Destiny said.

"Hey, Dee—" Mikey called. He slid off the raft. "Watch. I learned this stroke at day camp." He came splashing across the pool.

"Very nice," Destiny called.

"It was hot. I brought Mikey and Chris," Livvy said. "What's up?"

Destiny squatted down so she could talk quietly. She leaned over the pool. "Something bad happened, Liv. At the supermarket. I was almost caught. I—"

"I thought we were going to race," Mikey interrupted, holding on to the side of the pool.

"Not now. Dee and I are talking," Livvy said.

"You promised!" Mikey cried. He made a grab for Livvy's arm, missed. His hand bumped off her sunglasses, and they sank quickly to the bottom.

"Oops—!" Mikey started to laugh.

Destiny saw Livvy's eyes go wide. Her mouth dropped open. She grabbed at her eyes and started to moan.

"Nooooo! They're burning! Burning!"

Mikey gave her a shove. He laughed again. He always loved Livvy's dumb jokes.

But Destiny could see that her sister's pain was real.

Livvy pressed her hands tightly over her eyes. "Help me! Dee! My eyes! They're burning up!"

Destiny gripped Mikey's shoulders. "Dive down. Get her glasses."

Mikey dove down, his feet momentarily poking up over the surface. He came up with the sunglasses and shoved them into Livvy's hand.

Gasping loudly, her shoulders trembling, Livvy slid the glasses onto her face.

"Ha ha. Very funny," Mikey declared. He splashed a wave of water onto Livvy. "Your jokes are so stupid." He turned and floated back to his friend Chris.

Livvy gazed up at Destiny. "It . . . it's okay now. But . . . what happened?"

A feeling of dread swept over Destiny. "Livvy, our eyes—they can't stand the bright sun." She gasped. "And look at your skin. Did you put on sunscreen? You're totally sunburned."

Livvy gazed down at her arms and legs. "Oh, wow. I haven't been here more than half an hour! Dee, what does this mean?"

"We have to go," Destiny said. She climbed to her feet and called, "Mikey, Chris, out of the water now. Let's go."

"Aw, please—ten more minutes," Mikey whined.

"No. We have to go," Livvy said. She grabbed both his hands and tugged him to the steps. "You guys had a good swim."

Mikey splashed her again. "You're stupid. It was too short."

"Maybe I'll bring you back tomorrow," Destiny said. "Would you like that?"

"No."

Destiny found Mikey's beach towel and wrapped him up in it.

"Stop being such a grump," Livvy said.

"Make me."

Livvy turned and saw Chris come running toward them, his baggy swimsuit dripping water. "Do we really have to go?" Chris called. And then he slipped on the wet walkway and toppled heavily to the concrete.

"Ow!" He let out a cry and didn't move.

"Are you okay?" Livvy called. She ran to him. She dropped down beside him. "Chris?"

He sat up slowly. "My knee."

"You scraped it," Livvy said.

Destiny and Mikey hurried over to them.

"It's bleeding," Chris said, holding his leg.

Destiny stared at the blood, bright red even through her sunglasses. It glistened wetly on the bent knee.

Livvy leaned over, grabbed the boy's leg with both hands, and lowered her face to the knee.

"Livvy—don't," Destiny said softly.

But Livvy leaned lower and started to lick up the blood.

"Livvy—" Destiny called. "No—"

Livvy's tongue made rapid lapping sounds as her head bobbed over Chris's knee.

"What is she doing?" Mikey cried. "Why is she doing that?"

Chapter Fifteen

What Does Coach Bauer Know?

Livvy let go of Chris's knee and raised her head. Destiny could see the dazed expression on her sister's face.

"Why did you do that?" Mikey grabbed Livvy's shoulder. "What's your problem?"

Livvy stared up at him.

"It's a first-aid trick we learned at camp," Destiny told him, trying to keep her voice steady. "That's the fastest way to stop the bleeding." She turned to Chris. "How does it feel?"

"Okay."

Livvy helped Chris to his feet. "See? The bleeding's almost stopped. We'll put a bandage on it when we get home."

Destiny studied her brother. Did he believe her first-aid story? He was still watching Livvy warily.

Destiny turned and waved good-bye to Bree and Courtney. As the four of them made their way to the parking lot, Destiny saw the young man in black still standing in the shade. Still smiling.

Still watching her.

She looked away quickly.

What is *his* problem?

Up in their room, the door closed, Livvy grabbed Destiny's hand. "I couldn't stop myself. I suddenly felt so hungry. I saw the blood on Chris's knee, and—"

"Shhh." Destiny squeezed her sister's hand. "It's okay. I think they believed my first-aid story."

"But it's *not* okay. We're not okay. We . . . maybe we . . ." her voice trailed off.

"Maybe we were bitten by a vampire." Destiny finished the sentence for her. She felt a chill go down her back. "I've been thinking and thinking. Maybe at camp. It's the only place it could have happened."

Livvy let go of Destiny's hand and dropped onto her bed. "Dee, we've got to find someone to help us."

"Yes, we do," Destiny said. "And we may not have much time." She told Livvy what she had learned from Ari, about vampire hunters in

Dark Springs, about full-fledged vampires and neophytes.

"But isn't there an antidote?" Livvy whispered. "If we were bitten, isn't there something we can do to get back to normal? What did Ari say?"

Destiny shook her head. "Ari didn't know."

She told her sister about the supermarket incident, about the clerk running toward her, pointing and shouting. "I knew I'd been caught. I was in a total panic. He saw me drop the liver in my bag. I told him it slipped out of my hand. I said the package had come open. I said someone did a bad wrapping job and I got blood all over me."

"And did he believe you?"

Destiny nodded. "Yes. He started to apologize." She swallowed. "I was so scared, Liv. It was such a close call."

A heavy silence fell over them.

Livvy fingered the mark on her neck. "Maybe we *were* bitten. Maybe we're becoming vampires. I . . . I can't believe it. But maybe it's true."

She buried her face in her hands. "Do you really think there are hunters, Dee? Would they hunt us down and kill us if they found out about us?"

"Maybe," Destiny whispered. "I don't know."

"But we haven't done anything wrong," Livvy said with a sob. "It isn't our fault."

Destiny had the feeling that Livvy wanted to say more. She waited for her sister to continue, but Livvy sat in silence.

As Destiny reached to hug her sister, she had an idea. "Coach Bauer," she said aloud.

Livvy glanced up at her. "What about him?"

"Ari said Coach might be one of the vampire hunters. He might even be the leader. Maybe he knows about vampires, Liv. Maybe he could tell us what to do."

Livvy pulled away from Destiny. "Are you crazy? If Coach is one of the hunters, *no way* we can tell him what happened to us. He'll shove stakes through our hearts or something."

"Of course he won't," Destiny said softly. "Coach has known us since we were babies. He and Mrs. Bauer were at our house all the time. He's like family. He would never hurt us, Liv. And he might know something that would help us. I think we should go see him right away."

Livvy hesitated. "I'd be afraid, Dee. Really."

"Well, maybe we could tell him we're worried about a friend from camp. We just need information. He might know exactly what we should do."

"But, Dee, that's so lame."

"We're desperate, right? We have to try *something*—"

The phone rang. Destiny picked it up.

"Hi, Dee. It's Dad. How's it going?"

How's it going? Not exactly great, Dad.

"Everything's fine."

"Listen, dear, I won't be home till late. Two dogs got into a fight behind the playground. One of them had its eye clawed out. I think maybe if I'm lucky, I can put it back in."

"Yuck, Dad. That's really gross."

"Destiny, you're the animal lover in the family. If you want to be a doctor or a vet, you can't say things are gross."

"I guess."

"Anyway, can you feed yourselves? And take care of Mikey till I get back?"

"No problem, Dad."

"Thanks, kid. I love you. See you later."

Would you love me if you knew I suck down liver blood in the supermarket?

"Love you too, Dad. Bye." She turned to Livvy. "Dad won't be home till late."

"No problem," Livvy said. "I'll make my specialty for dinner."

"Your specialty? What's that?"

"Frozen pizza."

"Take off the crust for me," Mikey said.

"Can you wait? It isn't even out of the oven yet," Livvy replied. "And what's wrong with the crust?"

"Mom always cut off the crust for me," he said. And then his eyes went wide and his cheeks reddened. "Just cut it off, okay?"

Destiny stared at her little brother. "Mom cut off the crusts for you because she liked to eat them herself. She thought the crusts were the best part. You know, one night I caught her down here late at night eating a whole plate of pizza crusts."

She bent down and whispered in Mikey's ear, "It's okay to talk about Mom. You can talk about her any time you want to."

He looked at her. "Shut up," he snapped.

"Excuse me?"

"Just shut up." He stamped out of the kitchen.

Livvy peered into the oven window. "Almost ready."

Destiny pulled three dinner plates from the cabinet and carried them to the kitchen table. As she set out the plates, something on the bench against the window caught her eye. "Hey, what's that?"

She picked it up. A fat notebook, the cover scratched and worn, pages practically bursting out. She hoisted it onto one knee to flip through it. "Livvy, look—it's Coach Bauer's playbook. He must have left it here last night."

Livvy was lifting the pizza from the oven. "He'll come back for it."

"No. Don't you see? This is our excuse."

"You mean—"

"Our excuse to go see him tonight. We'll tell him we came to return the playbook. Then we'll tell him we've been hearing all these rumors about vampires, and maybe he'll tell us something to help us."

Livvy stared at the playbook. Destiny could see the fear on her sister's face.

"I'm frightened too," Destiny said. "I'm terrified. But we have to talk to someone. Coach Bauer might be our last hope."

Chapter Sixteen
Anyone Home?

Destiny's sneakers crunched over the gravel driveway. She clutched the playbook against the front of her sweatshirt. The wind, suddenly cold—a hint of fall days to come—gusted and swirled, shivering the old trees around the house, making them creak and groan.

"It's completely dark," Livvy whispered, a few steps behind Destiny. "I don't think he's home."

"He might be in back. We'll give it a try."

Destiny gazed up at the two-story shingle house. A loose shutter dangled from an upstairs window. Clumps of tall weeds poked over the front stoop. Beside the front window, a rhododendron bush lay withered on its side, flattened as if trampled.

"What a dump. The house used to look so nice when Mrs. Bauer was alive," Livvy whispered. "Remember? She was always bragging about her garden."

Destiny climbed onto the concrete stoop. She heard a dog barking, probably from the house across the street. A strong gust of wind nearly sent her tumbling off the stoop. No porch light. Her hand fumbled for the doorbell, finally found it, and pressed it.

"He's not home," Livvy whispered. She hugged herself. She wore a thin T-shirt.

"It's freezing out. How did it get so cold? We were just at the swimming pool. What crazy weather! Put on your coat right now." Destiny could hear her mother's voice.

She could picture Livvy stamping her feet, refusing to put on anything warm. It was the main thing Livvy and Mom argued about. It went on for years—the jacket war—and Mom never won once. Livvy was so stubborn, she'd walk to school through snow in just a T-shirt and jeans, just to win the battle.

She glimpsed her sister, shivering, hair blowing in the gusting wind.

At least *some* things never change.

No answer. Destiny pushed the bell again and held it down. She could hear the metallic ring on the other side of the door.

"He isn't here," Livvy said. "Let's go. I'm freezing."

Destiny put her ear to the door. No sounds inside the house. "We can't leave Coach's playbook out here on the stoop. Come on. The back door is probably open." Just about everyone in Dark Springs left their back doors unlocked. "We'll leave it for him in the kitchen."

Destiny led the way to the side of the house. She stepped around two bags of mulch stacked against the wall. One of the bags had come open, spilling its contents onto the grass. The bedroom windows were dark.

She turned the knob, and the kitchen door swung open easily. The girls stepped into the dark kitchen. Destiny closed the door behind them.

Livvy hugged herself. "It's nice and warm in here." She made a disgusted face. "Yuck. Smells like fish."

"Yes, it does," Destiny whispered. Then she called out, "Anyone home? Coach Bauer? Are you home?"

Silence. Destiny heard the clink of the ice maker inside the refrigerator.

She held the fat notebook in both hands.

"I'll leave it on the table," she whispered. "We'll have to come back, Liv. If he knows anything about vampires . . ."

She set the playbook down—and froze when she heard a groan nearby. "Did you hear that?" she whispered.

"Yes."

A creaking floorboard. Another groan.

Destiny gazed around the dark kitchen. Where's the light switch?

"Coach Bauer?" Her voice came out tight and shrill. "Coach? Is that you?"

A scraping sound. Loud breathing.

Someone is here. Someone is very close.

It has to be Coach Bauer. Why doesn't he answer?

"Coach? It's us—Destiny and Livvy."

Another muffled groan. From behind the door to the basement?

Destiny jumped as a hand grabbed her shoulder from behind. She cried out.

"Sorry," Livvy whispered. "I didn't mean to scare you. I . . . I don't like this. Let's get out of here."

"Okay."

But before she could move, Destiny heard

the creak of a door. She turned and watched with growing panic as the basement door slowly, slowly swung open.

"Coach? Is that you?"

Livvy tugged her arm. "Let's go!"

Destiny moved to the wall. She found the light switch and flicked on the kitchen lights.

"No! Oh, no!" She uttered a moan of horror as the pale, hollow-eyed figure stepped out from the basement. Clamping her hands to the sides of her face, Livvy opened her mouth in a high scream of terror.

Clinging to each other, the girls stared wide-eyed as the ghastly figure loomed closer.

"Mrs. Bauer!" Destiny shrieked. "It can't be. You're dead!"

"I'm not dead," Mrs. Bauer said in a hoarse whisper. "I am *undead*."

Chapter Seventeen
"He Won't Let Me Die"

Livvy gripped Destiny's arm so hard it hurt. Destiny gasped in horror as the woman moved toward them. Her bloodless face, the gray skin sagging over her jaw, the eyes sunken deep into the dark, round sockets, her skin peeling off, a patch of yellow bone visible beneath a hole in one cheek.

She used to be so beautiful. Mom always talked about how she wished she could look like Marjory Bauer.

"He . . . won't . . . let . . . me . . . die." The hoarse rasp rattled from deep in her throat. Every word seemed a struggle.

"Mrs. Bauer? Is it really you?" Livvy, hiding behind Destiny, finally found her voice.

"The poor man—he won't . . . let me die. He . . . can't . . . bear . . . to . . . part with me." Deep in their sockets, the gray eyes rolled up till only white was showing.

"He doesn't know how . . . selfish . . . he's being. I . . . want . . . to . . . *die*!"

"Mrs. Bauer—please—" Destiny staggered back, stumbling over Livvy.

"I . . . want . . . to . . . die, but he won't . . . let me!"

"Dee, look—look what she has in her hand," Livvy whispered.

Destiny lowered her gaze. Mrs. Bauer gripped a wooden stake in her hand, shaved to a point at one end.

"The poor man," Marjory Bauer continued. When she shook her hair, Destiny could see the skin tear at the back of her neck, a wide hole revealing gray tendons and yellow bone. "He keeps me here. But I want to die. Please? Please?" She raised the stake. She held it out to Destiny.

Destiny took another step back, into the kitchen counter. "Mrs. Bauer, what are you saying? How did this happen to you?"

"He keeps me in . . . the . . . basement," she continued, ignoring Destiny's questions. "He still wants me near him. But . . . I . . . can't . . . stand this life. Asleep all day . . . no light . . . never seeing the light. Forced to prowl . . . and to feed."

Again she raised the stake to Destiny. "Please? Please end it for me?"

"No!" Destiny cried. Her back pressed against the counter. She couldn't escape. "No, I can't, Mrs. Bauer."

Destiny glanced at her sister. Her eyes were wide with terror. She had backed up to the kitchen door and was fumbling for the knob.

"I'm sorry. I can't do it," Destiny told the woman. "I—I just came to return Coach's playbook. Livvy and I—we won't tell anyone about you. I promise. We'll keep your secret. We—"

Mrs. Bauer floated closer. She had Destiny trapped against the kitchen counter. She raised the stake one more time, and Destiny saw that the skin had fallen off her fingers, leaving only bone.

"You . . . won't help me . . . escape . . . this nightmare?"

"I'm sorry. No. I can't. Let me go. Please."

The sunken eyes rolled up in her head again. "Jenny took my dolly when I was five. Did you know that?"

Destiny swallowed. "I—I don't understand what you're saying."

Livvy motioned frantically for Destiny to

escape with her out the door. But Mrs. Bauer had Destiny pinned against the counter.

"Jenny took my dolly, so I had to buy a new one. I was only five. I cried and cried. I didn't want to play with Jenny anymore."

Oh my God. She's completely lost her mind.

Mrs. Bauer's eyes rolled down and locked on Destiny. "So hungry," she murmured through her blackened lips. "Always so hungry. I must feed now. That's why I awoke. I must . . . feed."

She loomed over Destiny . . . so close now, Destiny could smell her rotting skin. "Thank you . . . for coming, dear." Mrs. Bauer let the wooden stake drop from her hand.

"Mrs. Bauer, please. We won't tell anyone. I swear. I—"

"Thank you for coming. I'm hungry . . . so hungry. I must have blood. Now."

Her bony hands shot out fast. She caught Destiny by surprise. Destiny tried to squirm free, but the hands were strong, inhumanly strong. They wrapped around her head and tightened.

Destiny saw Mrs. Bauer's sunken eyes go wide with excitement. She saw the curled, yellow fangs slide down from the woman's blackened gums.

She tried to scream. She tried to pull free. But the bony hands held her in place.

Mrs. Bauer's sunken belly made a wet, gurgling sound. Destiny felt a wave of sour breath wash over her face as the woman dipped her head—and lowered her fangs to Destiny's throat.

Chapter Eighteen
Who Is the Restorer?

Destiny gave a final cry of protest and waited for the pain to shoot through her body. She felt Mrs. Bauer's dry tongue scrape against her skin. And then she heard the woman let out a startled gasp.

Mrs. Bauer pulled back her head. Her eyes, sunk so deep in the hollow cavities, stared at Destiny. "You too," she whispered.

Livvy grabbed Mrs. Bauer by the shoulders. "Let go! Let go of my sister!"

Mrs. Bauer drew back, stumbling over Livvy. She spun around and ran a bony finger along Livvy's throat. "You too," she whispered again. "You too. You too."

Livvy jumped away. Feeling the spot on her throat where Mrs. Bauer had touched her, Livvy edged beside her sister. "Let's go, Dee. Come on. Let's get out of here."

"You were bitten too," Mrs. Bauer

whispered. "I see the marks. And . . . I can . . . see it . . . in your eyes."

Trembling, still feeling the scrape of the woman's dry tongue on her skin, Destiny threw an arm around her sister's waist. "Wait. Don't run away," she whispered. "She won't harm us. Maybe she can help us."

"You have until . . . the next full moon," the woman rasped. "Not much time. Only a few weeks. Save yourselves. Save yourselves."

"But—how?" Destiny cried. "What do we do?"

"Only a few weeks," Mrs. Bauer repeated. She scratched her cheek and a chunk of skin fell off. "But . . . be careful. The hunters are out. The hunters . . . will find you."

"So it's true?" Destiny asked. "There *are* vampire hunters in Dark Springs?"

"Jenny took my dolly," Mrs. Bauer said, her eyes rolling up into her head. "Jenny took my dolly, so I pushed her in the mud. Her Sunday School dress was ruined. Ha ha."

"Mrs. Bauer, please," Destiny said. "Are there really hunters?"

"Jenny gave me a lollipop, but I hit her in the face with it."

"Can you help us?" Livvy cried. "Can you help us get back to normal?"

Mrs. Bauer moved quickly again. She lurched forward, grabbed Livvy's hand, and pinched the skin hard. "You're a lovely one. You don't want to be like me. Undead. Ha ha. What rhymes with undead?"

Livvy winced from the pain. She swung her arm, but the woman kept the tight grip on her hand. "Well, can you help us?" Livvy choked out.

"Have you seen . . . the Restorer?" Mrs. Bauer asked. She let go of Livvy's hand and turned to Destiny. "The Restorer is the one. He can . . . restore your life. Too late for me. He couldn't help me. But you . . . may have a little time."

Destiny's heart began to race. Was there really someone who could save them? Someone who could keep them from becoming like Marjory Bauer?

Her heart thudded in her chest. "Who is the Restorer? How can we find him?" she asked.

"Too late for Jenny," Mrs. Bauer said, shaking her head. "She fell off a horse and cracked her skull open. Good-bye, Jenny. I'm sorry I was so mean to you. I didn't know you would fall off your horse, did I?"

Destiny grabbed the woman's tattered sleeve. "Please. Tell us. How can we find the Restorer?"

"You need parental guidance. Guidance."

"Huh? Guidance? I don't understand," Destiny said.

"The hunters are coming," Mrs. Bauer replied. "They know who's been naughty and nice. They know. They're going to kill the naughty ones. But . . . they won't kill me. My husband . . . won't let them kill me. Please—kill me."

"Mrs. Bauer—the Restorer? Tell us."

"So hungry."

"Please?"

"So hungry. I must feed. You too. You too. You're one of them. You're one of us."

"Yes, but who is the Restorer?"

"So hungry." Mrs. Bauer spun away from them. Destiny could see the torn skin, the gaping hole in the back of her neck. The woman pulled open the door and disappeared into the night.

Destiny held on to her sister. A heavy

silence enveloped them, the only sound their rapid breathing.

"Is this really happening?" Livvy said finally.

"Let's go." Destiny pulled Livvy out the door. "Can you drive? I feel shaky."

"I guess."

Inside the car, Livvy dropped the key on the floor. She fumbled for it, then struggled to jam it into the ignition.

"Oh my God. That poor woman," Livvy said, shuddering. "Did you see what she looked like?"

"I'll never forget it. I'm going to have nightmares forever." Destiny grabbed Livvy's arm. "Look at me. I can't stop shaking. We can't let that happen to us, Liv. We can't! We have to find the Restorer. There isn't much time."

Destiny fiddled with the dashboard dials. "Can't we turn the heat up? I can't stop shivering."

"Destiny, there is no such thing as a Restorer. It was just crazy talk—like Jenny and the lollipop."

They drove home in silence. Dr. Weller's SUV was parked in the driveway. Through the windows, Destiny could see all the lights on in the house. Still shivering, she jogged to the back door.

Their dad greeted them at the door. In the harsh light on the porch, he looked tired, old. "I just got home a few minutes ago," he said softly. "There are some people here to see you."

Destiny and Livvy stared at each other. They both had the same thought.

The hunters!

Chapter Nineteen
Ari Strikes Out

Destiny gasped when she stepped into the living room and saw the visitors. Courtney, Fletch, and Ross sat on the floor, cheering Mikey on as he played a PlayStation racing game.

Courtney climbed to her feet. "Dee, hi. Why do you look so shocked?"

Destiny and Livvy exchanged glances. "We . . . uh . . . just didn't expect you," Destiny said.

"Where were you?" their dad asked. "I was surprised to find Mikey with Mrs. Mitchell next door."

"Uh . . . just doing some things," Destiny answered. Pretty lame. Could everyone see how upset and frazzled she was?

"Yeah. Things," Livvy echoed. Not helpful at all.

"Well, it's Mikey's bedtime," Dr. Weller said, scratching his graying hair. "How about it, Mikey?"

"How about *no way*?" Mikey replied, his fingers moving rapidly over the controller, his car rounding a turn on the video speedway.

Fletch used Mikey's shoulder to help push himself up from the floor. "Pretty cool game." He stretched his long arms over his head. "You guys want to go out or something?"

"I don't think so," Destiny said. "I'm . . . really tired."

Ross stood up. "It's only a few days till school starts. We've got to make the most of it. Who wants to go down to Donohue's, get some burgers, see if anyone else from school is hanging there?"

"I don't have any money," Courtney complained. "Someone has to treat me."

Fletch turned to her. "Hey, Court, we're always treating you. How come you never have any money?"

"Maybe it's because I'm poor?"

"Nice move, Fletch." Ross slapped his friend a low-five. "Got any other questions for her?"

"Give me a break." Fletch grabbed Ross and started wrestling around.

"Hey, cut it out, guys," Destiny said.

Please leave, everyone. Please. I'm so frightened, I can't think straight. I keep seeing that hideous woman . . . keep hearing her warnings rasping in my ears.

Ross held up a fifty-dollar bill, "Look— birthday money from my grandmother. I'll treat everyone at Donohue's."

Fletch put an arm around Ross's broad shoulders. "You the man!" He turned to Livvy. "You coming?"

Livvy crossed the room to Destiny. "Maybe we should go," she whispered. "You know. Help take our minds off . . . everything."

Destiny shook her head. "Not me. But if you think it will help you . . ."

Livvy had her eyes on Ross. "Yes. Maybe it will. . . ."

"Come on, you two," Courtney called from the front door. "Before Ross changes his mind."

Livvy turned and hurried after the others. She pulled her cell phone to her ear. "I'm calling Bree, guys. Maybe she'll want to meet us."

The door closed behind her. Destiny shut her eyes, enjoying the silence. But as soon as she closed them, she pictured Mrs. Bauer, her skin torn and decayed, her eyes tiny marbles sunk deep in her skull.

Destiny started to the stairs. Her dad stood

at the stove, waiting for the kettle to boil. He turned when he heard her enter. "Not going out with your friends?"

Destiny shook her head. "No. I'm kinda tired."

He narrowed his eyes at her, studying her.

Should I tell him what's happening to Livvy and me? Should I?

The teakettle on the stove whistled. He turned back to it.

Destiny hurried up the stairs to her room. She dropped down at her desk and clicked on the lamp. Then, elbows on the desktop, she buried her face in her hands.

This is a nightmare. I feel so helpless, so all alone.

I almost told Dad just now. But I can't do that. He looks so terrible, so old and sad. Besides, what could he do?

Destiny stepped to the mirror. She smoothed her fingers gently over the tiny puncture mark on her throat. Why doesn't it heal? She brought her face close to the glass.

What did Mrs. Bauer see in my eyes?

Yes. My eyes do look strange. My pupils are so tiny.

She picked up the phone and punched in Ari's number. He picked up after the third ring. "Ari, hey. It's me. What are you doing?"

"Dee—hi. I'm watching *Night of the Living Dead*. The 1990 version. I'm comparing it to the 1968 version. You know. The original."

"Which is better?" Destiny asked, trying to sound interested.

"The original, of course. The grainy black-and-white photography is so much more terrifying."

"Ari, can I ask you something? Remember what we were talking about this afternoon?"

"You mean vampires?"

"Yeah. Well, I have one more question. Have you—"

"How come you're so interested in vampires all of a sudden, Dee?" he asked.

He sounds suspicious, she realized. She felt her throat tighten.

"Hey—I know why!" he said. "I knew it! I knew it!"

Destiny nearly dropped the phone. *I should never have gone to see him. He's figured it out.*

"It's because you agree with me!" Ari

declared. "You agree that it's not a virus that killed those animals. It's vampires."

"Well . . . yeah." Destiny let out a long breath of air. "Right. And I . . . uh . . . want to learn as much as I can."

Whew.

"Cool," Ari said. "What were you going to ask me?"

"Well, have you ever heard of someone called the Restorer?"

Silence at the other end.

Then, "The Restorer? You sure you don't mean *The Regurgitator*? I remember a low-budget, independent film—totally gross—called *The Regurgitator*. This giant creature kept throwing up on Tokyo."

"No. It's not a movie," Destiny said impatiently. "I think it's supposed to be a real person."

"The Restorer?"

Come on, Ari. Please know who it is. Please come through for me.

"Is the Restorer a teacher?" Ari asked.

"Huh? Why do you say that?"

"I kinda remember some book I read on vampire lore. A long time ago. There was a teacher in it who claimed he could cure vampires. Is that what you mean?"

"Yeah. I guess. A teacher. . . . Can't you remember anything else?"

"No. Not really. I guess I struck out, Dee. You stumped me. You win the prize."

She sighed. "What's the prize?"

"Uh . . . you and me go to a movie tomorrow night?"

"What's *second* prize? No. I'm kidding. We'll have to see about tomorrow. Hey, I've got another call. Catch you later."

She clicked off the phone. She didn't have another call.

But she had to think. A teacher . . .

Mrs. Bauer had said *parental guidance*. And Ari had said a *teacher*.

Who else could help her? Who else might know about the Restorer?

Coach Bauer?

An image from her childhood flashed into her mind. She saw Coach Bauer looking much younger. Destiny remembered him tossing a football to Livvy and her. How old were they then? Seven or eight? Dad stood in the driveway, grinning, hands in his pockets. Barking out plays at the top of his lungs, Coach made the two girls run across the front yard, across the neighbor's yard, and heaved the ball high in the air at them.

Livvy always ducked. But sometimes Destiny would leap up and—miraculously—catch the ball. That made Coach cheer and jump up and down. When they went to toss it back, Bauer would warn them: "Don't throw like girls. Pull your arm back. Don't throw like girls."

Destiny loved Coach Bauer because he was the only adult who didn't treat her like a delicate little princess.

Thinking about those football games in the front yard, Destiny sobbed. Poor Coach. Hiding his undead wife in the basement, refusing to let her die. Forced to go out and hunt the vampires who ruined her life—and his.

The frightening thoughts circled her brain. Destiny slid over to her desktop computer. She pressed the power button and waited for it to go through its startup humming and beeping. Then she went online and called up Google.com.

She typed in *The Restorer* and *vampires*, and waited to see what the search engine found.

It took only a few seconds. Surprisingly, there was only one result.

But one will be enough if it's the right one!

Her hand trembling, Destiny clicked on the link. The website came up slowly. Destiny groaned when she read the large, blue headline at the top of the screen:

99% EFFECTIVE!
AMAZING HAIR RESTORER
GUARANTEED BY DOCTORS!

Disgusted, Destiny spun away from the computer.

Where else can I look?

She turned back to the screen—and discovered that she had an Instant Message:

Nak123: Hey, Dee. Izzat you?

Destiny leaned over the keyboard and typed.

Destiny1W: Nakeisha? What's up?
i miss you!

Nak123: I miss you too, girl.
And I miss camp. I think camp

should be 10 months and school
2 months in the summer.

Destiny1W: You got that right.
School start yet?

Nak123: Next week. Just hanging
out with friends. Baby-sitting
and stuff. You?

Destiny1W: Same. Hear from
anyone at camp?

Nak123: Not really. Planning my
college visits. You?

Destiny1W: Not yet.

Destiny hesitated. Did the vampire bite
Livvy and me at camp? Is that where it hap-
pened? Could anyone else have been bitten?
She took a deep breath and then typed.

Destiny1W: Hey, Nak—you been
feeling weird or anything since
u left camp?

Nak123: What kinda weird?

Destiny1W: Not normal-type
weird. I mean really STRANGE.

Holding her breath, Destiny waited for the answer. When it finally appeared, her mouth dropped open in shock.

Nak123: Yes. How did u know? i
change into a bat every night
and go flying around looking
for victims.

Chapter Twenty
Murdered

Whoa. Destiny stared at the words on the screen.

Is Nakeisha serious? Is she making a joke? I've got to know. . . .

```
Destiny1W: Me too. I capture
animals and drink their blood.

Nak123: That's what 8 weeks at
Camp Blue Moon will do to you.
I grew hair on my face and i
howl at the moon.

Destiny1W: lol
```

Nakeisha was joking. Destiny let out a sigh. The girls chatted online for a few more minutes. Nakeisha wrote that she'd be traveling with her mom this fall, looking at colleges, and they might drive through Dark Springs. Destiny replied that she couldn't wait to see her.

When she got offline, Destiny's eyelids felt heavy and her muscles ached. What a long, dreadful day, she thought, yawning.

Stretching, she walked to the open window and peered down on the front yard. Snakes of black cloud rolled over the pale half moon. The yard lay in deep shadow. A car rolled past slowly, one taillight out. Destiny could hear the music on its car radio.

Destiny squinted hard and saw a gray squirrel with a nut in its mouth, darting across the grass.

I can hear it. I can hear the squirrel's footsteps.

Destiny clapped her hand to her mouth. She suddenly felt sick. Her stomach lurched. She fought to keep her dinner down.

I'm changing. My body is changing. My hearing is becoming . . . inhuman. Oh my God. I can hear a squirrel's footsteps.

She shut her eyes and listened hard. Concentrated.

She could hear breathing. Mikey, asleep, breathing slowly, steadily, in his room downstairs.

And she could hear her dad, humming softly to himself, probably reading a book in bed. His stomach growled. She could hear his stomach growl all the way up in her garage room!

Where is Livvy?

Livvy and I have *got* to talk. We don't have time to waste.

She picked up the phone and punched in Livvy's cell number. Livvy answered on the second ring. "Where are you?" Destiny asked.

"You know. Donohue's."

"Well, come home now. We've got to talk."

"But it's still early, Dee."

"No. Come home, Liv. Right now. There's no time for hanging out with friends. We've got to make a plan."

Livvy hesitated. Destiny could hear the crowd at the restaurant, the steady thump of the reggae music on the stereo there. "Okay. Be right home. Promise."

Destiny clicked off the phone. She won't come for another hour or two. I know her. I'd better go get her.

She pulled on her denim jacket, brushed her hair, found her sneakers. Then she crept out of the house.

She stepped out into a cool, cloudy night. The wind gusted, sending dead leaves swirling off the ground in wide circles. Donohue's was just five or six blocks toward town. Destiny zipped her jacket and started to jog.

Three blocks from home, she saw a figure walking toward her on the sidewalk. "Livvy!"

"Hi," her sister called. "What are you doing out here?"

"Coming for you," Destiny answered, breathing hard from her run.

Livvy frowned. "I told you I'd be right home."

Destiny shrugged. "I just wanted to get some air."

"I'm a little worried about Bree," Livvy said.

"How come?"

"Well, she said she was coming to meet us. But then she never showed. I tried her cell, but . . . no luck."

"Weird," Destiny muttered.

They turned and started walking toward home. The moon kept sliding behind clouds, then reappearing, making it seem as if the pale light over the lawns and houses kept turning on and off.

"Can you hear it?" Destiny asked. "Can you hear every leaf rustling? Can you hear bugs crawling in the trees?"

Livvy's mouth dropped open. "Yes. Yes, I can, Dee. It's . . . terrifying. Every sound so clear. As if the whole world is closing in on us or something."

As if we're some kind of animals, Destiny thought. Some kind of night creatures.

Destiny pointed. "Hey, what's that?"

They had reached the vacant lot just cleared next to the corner house. Destiny squinted at something on the ground beside a large backhoe. Was it a pile of rags the workmen had left behind?

No. The clouds parted. Moonlight washed over the lot, revealing a pale, white leg.

No. Two legs, gleaming so brightly against the darkness of the ground.

Destiny's eyes focused on the pile of blond hair, silvery in the pale light from above. And then the whole scene faded like a dream, and the sprawled, still figure appeared to sink into the ground as clouds covered the moon and darkness spread again.

"Oh, no. Bree!" Livvy let out a choked whisper and took off running, her sneakers thudding the ground, hair bouncing behind her. Destiny took a deep breath and hurried after her.

Please, no.

But, yes. It was Bree.

She wore a short skirt and a brown leather jacket. She lay on her back, legs spread, one arm bent beneath her body. Her thick hair covered her face.

"Bree? Bree?" Livvy shouted her name in a high, shrill voice. "Bree? It's me." She dropped down beside Bree and began smoothing the hair off her friend's face.

"Bree? Bree? It's Livvy. Bree?"

Breathing hard, Destiny stood behind Livvy, staring down at the unmoving girl. Bree's eyes were open. They gazed up blankly, wide with horror. Her lipsticked mouth was open, as if frozen in a scream.

"Bree? Please move. Please!" A sob escaped Livvy's throat. "She's . . . dead. She's dead, Dee. Oh my God, she's dead."

Chapter Twenty-One
Destiny's New Neighbor

Moonlight washed over them again. Destiny blinked as Bree went out of focus, pale skin glowing in the light. And then Destiny's eyes stopped at the dark stain on Bree's gleaming throat.

Oh, no.

Destiny stooped beside her sister and narrowed her eyes at the spot. She reached out a trembling hand and smoothed her finger over Bree's throat. The skin felt so cool and soft.

Two tiny puncture wounds. Dark droplets of blood clinging to the holes.

Someone drank her blood.

Someone drank all her blood and killed her.

Livvy raised her head and stared through her tears at Destiny. "Dee, how long have you been out here?"

Destiny's mouth dropped open. The question stunned her. "Huh? What do you mean?"

"Did you get the hunger again?" Livvy demanded, holding Bree's lifeless hand. "Did you, Dee? Did it happen again?"

Destiny gasped and staggered back. "Are you accusing me? Livvy, are you accusing me? Have you gone crazy?"

Livvy stared up at her, tears rolling down her face. She let Bree's hand fall to the grass. She jumped to her feet, sobbing loudly.

"I—I'm sorry," Livvy said through her tears. "I'm sorry, Dee. I didn't mean it." She threw her arms around Destiny and held her tight, pressing her hot, wet cheek against her sister's.

"I'm sorry. I'm sorry."

"It's okay," Destiny whispered. "I understand. It's okay."

But it wasn't okay.

My own sister, accusing me of murder.

What next?

Destiny stepped out of the house, pumping her legs high, trying to stretch her muscles. A light rain was falling, but she didn't care. She had to get out.

She jogged down the driveway and turned right, heading to Drake Park three blocks down.

She turned her Red Sox cap around to let the rain hit her face. The cold raindrops felt soothing on her hot forehead.

Three days of pounding rain, and so much sadness.

Bree's funeral, with the wind tearing at the black umbrellas. The gravesite—the deep, rectangular hole—half filled with brown mud. Rain pattering the dark wood coffin. Like tears. Like tears raining down from the charcoal sky.

Was Bree really inside that coffin? It seemed so impossible.

I'll never forget Livvy's sobs. Dad's grim face. His head bent so low on his shoulders as if it was broken. His hand on my shoulder. I'll never forget how light it felt, the warmth filtering through my dark blouse.

And Coach Bauer so pale and tight-lipped, head bowed, sitting by himself in the last row of the church. I watched him during the service. He never looked up. Was he thinking about Marjory, his wife? Was he thinking that in her hunger she had murdered Bree?

And Bree's mother, her cries echoing off the church walls. "Why? Why did this happen? Somebody tell me!" she screamed. She collapsed beside the casket and had to be helped away.

And as the minister spoke, the sobs in the room drowned out the organ music. . . .

The rain stopped, but drops still fell from the trees. Destiny crossed the street and, running hard, made her way into the park. Her shoes splashed up waves of water from the puddled ground. Behind her, a car horn honked, but she didn't turn around.

I want to run till I'm exhausted. I want to run till I can't think anymore.

But the cool wet air made her more alert, made her thoughts clearer, sharper. The soft thuds of her steps rang in her ears. But she could also hear the scamper of rabbits and squirrels under the trees. She could hear the trickle of water in Drake Creek, the shallow bed of brown water on the far side of the park. She heard a chipmunk's light footsteps as it burrowed through the wet grass.

Destiny pressed her hands over her ears.

I can't stand this. I have to get my life back.

"Hello." A young man stepped out from behind a tree.

"Oh!" Destiny cried out.

He had a warm smile. "I'm so sorry. I didn't

mean to startle you."

Destiny squinted at him. I've seen him before. Where have I seen him?

He wore a long black trench coat open over a tan sweater and tan slacks. His wavy black hair was slicked straight back.

"I love walking here," he said. "It's so peaceful." He had a slight foreign accent.

Destiny nodded. "Yeah. No one uses this park much."

He came closer. He stared into her eyes without blinking. "Do you live nearby?"

Destiny motioned with her head. "A few blocks."

Is he nearsighted? Why the intense stare?

"I'm new here," he said. "I just moved a few weeks ago."

Destiny shoved her hands into the pockets of her rain slicker. "Do you like it here?"

A smile spread over his handsome face. "Oh, yes. Very much. And I'm going to like it a lot more in just a few weeks."

Destiny blinked. "A few weeks?"

He nodded. He kept his intense gaze on her as he stepped closer.

He's starting to creep me out, she decided.

He's really good-looking, but there's something about him . . .

"I've gotta go," she said.

But he grabbed her by the shoulders and held her in place. "Don't go, Laura. I don't want you to leave." His eyes burned into hers.

Destiny gazed into them, unable to look away.

"Waiting is so hard for me," he said. "I watch the moon every night, and I think about you. I think about us and how happy we'll be in a few weeks."

Destiny heard the trickle of the creek and the rustle of the leaves in the trees. But she couldn't hear his words. What was he saying to her?

He pulled her to him and pressed his face against hers. "Having you so close to me, Laura . . . I can hardly bear it."

His face felt cold against her cheek. She struggled to hear what he was saying. But it was lost in a steady rush of wind.

"I'm going to stay close to you," he whispered, his dry lips brushing her ear. "I'll be where I can see you every day. And when the time comes . . . when the time comes, my love, *you* will come to me. You will come to me and drink my blood. Then you will be mine forever."

The trees with their fading leaves tilted and swayed above Destiny's head. She felt so dizzy, so weak.

"I'm sorry. I can't resist any longer," he whispered. He pulled back his head, his black eyes glowing.

Destiny struggled to look away. But she couldn't turn. She couldn't move. His eyes were black tunnels, endless, leading nowhere.

He pulled open her rain slicker. He tugged down the neck of her sweatshirt. His mouth opened to reveal curled, yellowed fangs.

"Can't wait any longer . . . can't wait." He lowered his head.

Destiny felt a pinprick of pain at her throat.

She couldn't move, couldn't breathe. Her eyes were as clouded as the sky. But she could see his dark, curly hair beneath her chin . . . see his head bob up and down at her throat as he drank . . . drank . . . drank.

Chapter Twenty-Two

"You Didn't Like Bree"

"What's up?" Livvy turned away from the makeup mirror on her dressing table as Destiny entered their room. "Where've you been?"

"Drake Park," Destiny said. She pulled off the yellow rain slicker and tossed it onto her bed. Her arms and legs ached. She felt so weary. "I went for a run."

Livvy squinted at her. "In the rain?"

Destiny sat down on the bed and pulled off her wet, muddy sneakers. "I just had to get some fresh air. How are you doing?"

Livvy shoved tubes and jars of makeup away. "Not great. I can't stop thinking about Bree. I just can't get my mind off her."

Destiny crossed the room and put her hands on her sister's shoulders. "It's hard. I think about her too. I guess it will just take time."

Livvy's expression turned cold. "You never liked her."

"Huh?"

"I know you didn't. You thought she was a bad influence. Because she was so . . . different. She always did what she wanted to. She didn't care what people thought of her."

Livvy's eyes locked on Destiny. "You thought she was slutty. You thought she was cheap—didn't you! You hated it because I started spending more time with her."

"Livvy, listen. I didn't—" The words caught in Destiny's throat.

"It was so obvious how much you resented Bree."

"Listen to me," Destiny shouted. "Being angry at me isn't going to help. I know you're angry that your friend is dead. But taking it out on me isn't going to bring her back. You and I, we have to—"

"What's that?" Livvy interrupted. She raised a finger to Destiny's throat. "You're bleeding."

"What?" Destiny leaned into the mirror. "Oh, no." Her heart started to pound as she stared at the two red droplets of blood on her throat. Livvy handed her a tissue, and she wiped the blood away.

And now Destiny stared at the two red marks, the tiny cuts in her skin. Fresh red cuts.

Livvy jumped to her feet and angrily shook Destiny. "I knew you've been keeping secrets from me. You didn't go for a run. Where have you been? Tell me the truth. What were you doing?"

"I . . . don't know," Destiny stammered.

"Tell me how this happened," Livvy demanded.

Destiny stared in horror at her reflection. "I can't. I can't explain it, Liv. I did go for a run and—"

"It's not true!" Livvy cried. "You're doing something. You're doing something and not telling me!"

"Livvy, listen to me. Please!"

Livvy's hands were balled into tight fists. "No! You listen to me. I believe what you said, that you didn't kill Bree. But you were there, Dee. You were right there where she was murdered, and you had no reason to be. And now . . . you come home with bite marks on your throat. And you won't tell me the truth about it."

"I don't *know* the truth!" Destiny cried.

"Yes, you do! What are you doing? *What are you doing?*"

Destiny reached to hug her sister, but Livvy pulled away. "You're hysterical. You're not thinking clearly!" Destiny cried. "You have to believe me. I'm not doing anything behind your back, Liv. I'm in the same mess you're in and—"

"*You* didn't lose your best friend," Livvy said through clenched teeth. She slammed her fist on the dressing table, sending tubes and bottles flying. Then she spun away and stomped down the stairs, slamming the front door behind her.

Destiny leaned close to the mirror and studied the fresh marks on her neck. Her hand trembled as she rubbed a finger over them. Her whole body shook.

"Livvy, don't leave me now," she whispered. "I need you more than ever."

The doorbell rang.

Chapter Twenty-Three
A Death in the Family

Destiny hurried down to the front door and pulled it open. "Ross—hi!"

She realized she had her hand over the fresh red wounds. She lowered it slowly, adjusting the top of her sweatshirt.

Ross stepped into the house. He wore a blue-and-red Red Sox jacket over faded jeans. "How's it going, Dee?"

"Not great. How about you?"

"About the same. Hold still." Ross reached out and pulled something from her hair. He showed it to her—a curled, wet leaf.

"I was running. In the park," she said, smoothing back her hair. "You know. To get some fresh air. Time to think."

He nodded. "Fletch and I got a basketball game together at the playground this morning just to take our minds off things. We played in the rain. We didn't care."

She led him into the kitchen. "What's up?"

He pulled up a kitchen stool. "I was over at Courtney's. She had to leave for her tennis lesson."

She poured out two glasses of orange juice and handed him one. "I talked to Courtney this morning. You know how scared she gets at Ari's movies. Now she says she's terrified to leave her house at night."

"Yeah. I tried to cheer her up." He took a long drink.

"Courtney has always been such a scaredy-cat. Remember when we were little and a bunch of us went behind her garage and made scary noises and howls, and we convinced her that her garage was haunted? And for weeks, she was too terrified to go in it and get her bike?"

"That was before I moved here," Ross said. "How come you were all so mean to Courtney?"

Destiny shrugged. "Kids are mean, I guess. And Courtney was always such a good victim."

The word *victim* hung in the air between them. Destiny wished she hadn't said it. She sighed. "School starts on Monday. It's our big-deal senior year. No one feels like going."

"Did you see the paper this morning?

They're calling the guy who murdered Bree the Vampire Killer. Because her blood was totally drained. The police say it's some kind of sick maniac."

Destiny blinked. *Sick maniac.* She rubbed a finger over the tiny wound on her throat. *Sick maniac.*

Did the same sick maniac bite me? Does he plan to kill me too? Why can't I remember? Why?

"So they don't think it's a virus anymore?" Destiny asked, struggling to clear her head.

"No," Ross replied. "They dropped the virus story. They think it's some twisted sicko who started with animals and now has moved on to people."

Destiny nodded, trying not to reveal her fear.

"I heard there might be a curfew in town," Ross continued. "Everyone has to be inside by ten o'clock."

"Maybe they'll catch the guy," Destiny said softly.

"Maybe it's a real vampire," Ross said, spinning the glass between his hands.

She stared at him. "Now you sound like Ari."

"Ari could be right about this. No joke. But

if it's a real vampire, there are people in town ready to deal with him."

Destiny narrowed her eyes at Ross. "You mean . . . the hunters?"

His eyes widened. "You've heard of them?"

Destiny moved closer to him. "What do you know about them?"

Ross shrugged. A strange smile crossed his face. "Nothing, really. Just rumors."

"Ross, have you ever heard of the Restorer?" Destiny blurted out.

He finished his orange juice. "Restorer? You mean *paint* restorer or something?"

"No. The Restorer has something to do with vampires." She looked at him eagerly.

Please—know something.

Ross shook his head. "No. I never heard of that." He studied her. "How come you're asking about that?"

She could feel herself blushing. "It's just something Ari was talking about."

Ross raised his eyes to the hallway. "Is your dad home? I actually came to see him."

"Dad?" Destiny couldn't keep the surprise from her voice. "Dad's at his office. He's been working six days a week. But he said he'd be home early today. If you want to wait."

"Well . . ."

"Why'd you want to see Dad?"

Ross scratched his short hair. "My dog is sick. I wanted to ask him about it."

"Sparky? What's wrong with him?"

Ross hesitated. "I don't know really. He's throwing up and stuff."

Destiny studied him. He seemed so uncomfortable, not like Ross at all. She had a strong feeling he was lying about the dog. But why would he lie?

"Think he'll be home soon?" he asked.

Destiny nodded. "You can help me with a project while you wait."

"Project?"

"I convinced Dad the garage needs to be painted. He's been in such a daze, the whole house is falling apart. I'm trying to snap him out of it. So, he said he'd paint the garage if I drag everything out and pile it on the side of the house. You can help me."

Ross rolled his eyes. "Sounds awesome."

"Oh, come on. It won't take long." She pulled him out to the garage.

They started with the bikes and gardening

equipment. Then Ross dragged out heavy bags of peat moss and planting soil. They talked about friends and school starting and the summer, and carefully avoided mentioning Bree.

He's such a great guy, Destiny thought. I like him so much. She pictured him with his arms around her . . . kissing her.

"You're so different from your sister," Ross said. His cheeks turned pink. They were carrying out Mikey's bike and a bright-yellow plastic Mercedes that he pedaled around in when he was three.

"Different? How do you mean?" Destiny asked.

Before Ross could answer, a voice called from the garage door. "Hey, you two, what's up?"

Ross's eyes went wide. "Livvy, hi."

Livvy wore a blue vest and a tight, cropped pink-and-blue T-shirt and a pair of low-slung jeans. She ignored Destiny. Her eyes were on Ross. "Why are you cleaning out the garage? You moving in?"

He set down the carton he'd been carrying. "Destiny asked me to help."

"I think Dad asked *you* to help too," Destiny said to Livvy. She didn't mean to sound so shrill, but she was unhappy that Livvy had barged in just when she and Ross were starting to really talk.

Livvy walked over to Ross and pulled a clump of dust off his shoulder. She gave him a sexy smile. "Want to take a little break?"

Ross turned back to Destiny. "We got a pretty good start."

Destiny nodded. "Yeah, thanks. It was really nice of you to help out."

Livvy pulled him out the door and to the side of the garage. Destiny heard them giggling about something. She decided to take a break too. Brushing off the front of her jeans, she started toward the house.

She pretended she didn't see Livvy and Ross. Livvy had him backed against the garage wall. His arms were around her waist. Her hands were pressed against his cheeks, her head was tilted to one side, and she was kissing him, a long, passionate kiss.

Destiny turned away and ran into the house.

Livvy and Ross remained at the side of the garage for about half an hour. From the kitchen window Destiny watched Ross leave. Then she grabbed Livvy as she entered the kitchen. "You and I have to talk."

Livvy glared at her. "Can I get something to drink first?"

Livvy grabbed a can of iced tea from the fridge, popped the top, took a long drink, then followed Destiny up the stairs to their room.

"I don't understand why you're not helping," Destiny said. She couldn't keep her voice from trembling.

Livvy stared at her. "Helping with the garage?"

"No. You know what I'm talking about. Helping to find a way to save us. Helping to find the Restorer. You just pretend that we've got all the time in the world."

Livvy sighed. "What are we supposed to do? Look him up in the phone book?"

"We have to do everything we can," Destiny replied. "We have so little time. I've been through every book in the library about vampires and the supernatural. I've gone through website after website. I called someone in the science department at the junior college. I had another long talk with Ari, but he's starting to get suspicious. I'm so desperate, I even called a supernatural-phenomenon hotline I saw advertised in a magazine."

"And?" Livvy asked.

Destiny frowned. "Nothing. No mention anywhere. No one has heard of anything called the Restorer. No clue. Livvy, I'm so terrified."

"Think I'm not?" Livvy replied.

"But you're not helping me," Destiny said. "You're pretending it's all going to be okay. But it isn't. We have maybe a week or two at the most. We can't let the days go by like this. You've been acting strange, Liv. Ever since Bree died, you've been so angry at me."

Livvy lowered her head. Her hair fell over her face, but she made no attempt to push it away. "Okay, okay. What do you want me to do?"

"The first thing is, we have to stick together. We can't let things drive us apart." Destiny thought of Ross. She forced him from her mind.

"We can't give up, Liv," she continued. "We have to do whatever we can to find this Restorer. We'll go back to Mrs. Bauer. She knows more than she told us. We'll go back there. We'll find out what we need to know, and we'll save ourselves."

A sob escaped Livvy's throat. She tore at the sides of her hair. "How can there be any hope? I lost my best friend. And I'm thirsty. I'm thirsty all the time. I'm not getting enough blood, Dee. I'm not!"

Destiny put an arm around her sister's shoulders. "We'll find the Restorer in time. I know we will. I know—"

A high, shrill scream made Destiny jump.

"Help me!"

Mikey's cry from downstairs.

Both sisters scrambled to the stairway.

"Eddy's dead!" They heard Mikey scream. "Eddy's dead! Help me! My hamster is dead!"

Destiny turned and stared at Livvy.

Livvy spun away. "I couldn't help it," she whispered. "I was thirsty."

Chapter Twenty-Four
The Hunters Are Here!

Their dad called while they were still calming Mikey down. Destiny picked it up.

"I've got to work late. I've got two cats here that need stomach operations. Can you girls take care of Mikey tonight?"

"Sure, Dad. No problem. But I'm worried about you. You're working late every night. When are you going to take a break?"

Destiny heard her father sigh. "Beats me. When animals stop getting sick, I guess. See you later, Dee." He clicked off.

Destiny stared at the phone. Mom could always force Dad to come home. I know he cares about us. But why does he want to spend all of his time in his lab now?

She turned to Livvy. "Dad's going to be late. He wants us to watch Mikey."

"But what about Mrs. Bauer?"

"I have an idea." She punched in Ana-Li's

number. "Hey, Ana-Li. It's Destiny. Can you stay with Mikey for an hour or two?"

"Sure," Ana-Li replied. "What's up? Why can't you and Livvy watch him?"

"Uh . . . Dad wanted us to run some errands. You know. Supplies he needs. He can't get away from the office."

Pretty lame. Will she buy it?

"No prob. I'll be right over."

Destiny turned back to Mikey. "You feeling any better?"

"No," he grumbled. He gazed from Livvy to Destiny. "Will you die too?"

Stunned by the question, Livvy gasped. "What on earth?"

Destiny understood. The poor kid. He lost his mom and then his pet. He knew about Bree. So much death this year.

"Livvy and I aren't going to die," she said softly. "We're going to stay with you, Mikey. And we'll always take care of you."

He stared back at her, studying her.

I hope I'm telling him the truth.

Poor Mikey. Poor Mikey. If we don't find the Restorer, he could lose us too.

She turned away quickly to keep him from seeing the tears in her eyes.

* * *

The car headlights bounced off the fog, sending shafts of yellow light shooting in all directions. Destiny drove slowly, leaning over the steering wheel. The sky was solid black, and the fog rolled over the car as if swallowing it.

Livvy was hunched low in the passenger seat, knees on the dashboard, arms crossed tightly in front of her black sweater. "I can't believe you're dragging me back there," she whispered.

Destiny slowed for a stop sign. "Do we have a choice? I told you, I've been doing research day and night. And I haven't found any clues. Not one."

"But this woman is . . . a vampire. She's crazy. She's totally out of her head. She could be really dangerous."

Destiny lowered her foot on the gas. "She won't harm us, remember? She said we were almost vampires too. You keep forgetting that part."

Livvy touched the mark on her throat. "We're doomed, Dee. That crazy woman is not going to help us."

"She *has* to help us," Destiny insisted. "No more negative talk. She *has* to help."

She pulled the car to the foot of the driveway. Coach Bauer's house stood in darkness, half hidden by the curtain of fog. It looked unreal to Destiny, like a movie set of a haunted house.

It *is* haunted. By a woman who's not alive and not dead.

"Turn on the flashlight. I can't see a thing," Livvy whispered as they made their way up the driveway.

"No. No light till we get inside," Destiny said. "We don't want anyone to see us."

"Ow." Livvy tripped over a large rock at the side of the house and stumbled into the shingled wall.

"Careful," Destiny whispered, gripping Livvy's shoulder and helping her to stand upright. "I don't see any lights in the house. Coach isn't home."

"Probably out with his hunters, killing all the vampires in town," Livvy muttered.

"Shhh. Stop. This is freaky enough."

"What if Mrs. Bauer isn't here? What if she's out flying around, killing some of our other friends?"

Destiny stopped short and held Livvy back. "Pull yourself together," she said. "Stop whining. And stop acting like a child and forcing me to be the grownup."

Livvy opened her mouth to protest, but changed her mind.

"Just remember why we're here," Destiny said. "To find out about the Restorer." She carefully pulled open the back door. She poked her head into the dark kitchen. "Anybody home?" she called softly.

Silence.

The cold of the fog clung to her as she stepped into the warm kitchen. She rubbed the back of her neck, trying to smooth the dampness away. Then she clicked on the flashlight.

She sent the circle of light dancing over the room. Dishes were piled in the sink. An empty Hungry-Man dinner box sat on the counter beside two empty beer bottles.

She moved the light to the basement door. The door stood open a crack. Had Mrs. Bauer escaped? Was she out on the prowl?

"Come on," Destiny whispered.

Livvy hovered close behind as Destiny followed the beam of light to the basement door. Destiny pulled the door open slowly. "Anyone there?" she called down.

Silence.

Destiny could hear the hum of the refrigerator. Somewhere outside, far down the block, a car horn honked.

Keeping the light on the stairs, Destiny led the way. The wooden steps creaked and groaned as the girls made their way to the basement.

Destiny stopped at the bottom to catch her breath. If only she could slow her racing heart.

"Where is she? Is she down here?" Livvy stood so close, Destiny could feel her hot breath on the back of her neck.

Destiny moved the circle of light slowly around the cluttered basement. It swept over rows of cartons stacked three high. Past an old couch. Past a large black steamer trunk with a big lock clasped to the front.

The light stopped on a narrow bed against the far wall. First Destiny saw the dark quilt that covered the bed. Then she saw the head on the pillow. Mrs. Bauer!

"At least she doesn't sleep in a coffin," Destiny murmured.

"You've seen too many of Ari's movies," Livvy whispered.

Destiny's legs began to tremble, but she forced them to take a few steps toward the sleeping woman. Suddenly, Mrs. Bauer cringed, let out an angry cry, and shielded her eyes with the back of a bony hand.

Destiny lowered the flashlight. She hadn't even realized she had flashed it into the woman's face.

With a groan, Mrs. Bauer raised herself to a sitting position. She rubbed her sunken eyes, deep in their round sockets. Scraggly hair fell over her face.

"Who is it? Have you come for me?" Her voice came out muffled, as if from somewhere far away. Her bony hands and arms trembled in front of her. "Who are you?"

"It's . . . us again," Destiny managed to whisper. "The Weller twins."

The woman tilted her head one way, then the other. "I used to know a twin, but she died."

Destiny's throat felt dry. She realized her hands were trembling. "Mrs. Bauer, we don't want to disturb you. We just want to ask you—"

"I knew a twin, but she died . . . she died . . . she died . . ." Mrs. Bauer sang the words in a hoarse sing-song.

"We want to ask you one question. Then we'll leave," Destiny said.

"I'm so hungry," the woman rasped. She

stood up, the dark quilt tangled around her long black shift. "So hungry."

"Who is the Restorer?" Livvy asked, clinging close to Destiny. "Please—tell us. Who is the Restorer?"

The woman tilted her head from side to side again. "So close," she whispered. "So close."

"What is so close?" Destiny demanded. "The Restorer? The Restorer is so close?"

"Hungry," Mrs. Bauer murmured. She stuck a finger deep into her eye socket and pulled out a dead fly. "Hungry. So close."

"Is the Restorer close?" Destiny pleaded. "Please—tell us. We need to know who the Restorer is."

"You know, don't you?" Livvy asked. "Don't you? Can you tell us?"

"He . . . couldn't . . . restore me," the woman replied. "He tried. It was . . . too . . . late. Too late for me."

"So you know the Restorer. Where can we find him?" Destiny asked again. "*Please*—tell us."

"So close. So close."

Destiny held her breath, waiting for Mrs. Bauer to say more.

"Tell us!" Livvy pleaded. "Tell us!"

A heavy thud above their heads made all three of them jump. With a gasp, Mrs. Bauer stumbled back against the wall.

Destiny heard a door slam upstairs. Then more heavy thuds. Footsteps. Rapidly crossing the kitchen floor.

"The hunters!" Mrs. Bauer whispered, sunken eyes rolling wildly in their sockets. "They've come. They've found me."

Destiny swallowed hard. "The hunters? They've come here to—"

"To kill me," Mrs. Bauer said. She had her hands at the sides of her head, tugging at her patchy hair. "To kill me."

Livvy grabbed Destiny's arm. "Hurry. We have to get out of here. They'll wonder why we're here with her. And if they check our throats and see the marks, they'll kill us too."

The door to the basement swung open. Destiny heard men's voices, talking rapidly, excitedly. The bright beam of a flashlight swept down the stairs.

Destiny spun around, her eyes circling the basement. "There's no way out, Liv," she whispered. "No way out. We're trapped."

Chapter Twenty-Five

"Come and Get Me!"

Livvy pressed her hands against her cheeks, her features tight with fear. Destiny grabbed Mrs. Bauer's bony arm. "Is there a way out? Can we get out?"

"They've come," Mrs. Bauer replied, her eyes on the stairs. "The hunters have finally come."

Squinting into the darkness, Destiny saw a stairway along the far wall. Did it lead to a door to the outside?

Yes.

"Hurry." Destiny let go of Mrs. Bauer and broke for the stairway. She heard Livvy running close behind. Destiny scrambled up the steep stairs on all fours, then reached up and pushed the metal door open a crack.

She let out a happy cry as the night sky came into view. Using all her strength, she pushed the door open and scrambled up and onto the grass.

Then she turned and helped pull Livvy up. She could hear footsteps crossing the basement. Men's voices. Cries and shouts.

Destiny squinted through the fog. Beyond the low shrubs at the back of the yard, she could see the black silhouettes of trees. The woods. "Let's go."

She and Livvy took off, running full speed, shoes slipping over the dew-wet grass. As they neared the trees, Destiny glanced back—and saw Mrs. Bauer climbing out of the basement.

Mrs. Bauer scrambled to her feet and began to lurch toward the trees. "Come and get me!" she shouted. "Come and get me!" Her black shift flapped in the wind. Her scraggly hair flew around her skeletal face.

Destiny and Livvy reached the safety of the trees. They ducked down beside each other, hiding in the darkness. Breathing hard, they peered back to the yard.

Bright halogen lanterns sent wide circles of white light over the grass. The lanterns swept over the ground, bright as day, lighting the figures pursuing Mrs. Bauer, trapping her in harsh spotlights.

Holding on to the rough bark of a tree,

Destiny could see their hooded sweatshirts, hear their shouts.

"Livvy—that tall one—is that Coach Bauer?"

"I don't know. I think so."

"And those guys shouting to each other. Oh my God. I think I recognize their voices. Aren't those guys from the basketball team?" Destiny whispered.

Livvy stared straight ahead. "I . . . I think so. Is Ross there? Has he become a hunter? Oh no. Why didn't he tell us?"

Destiny grabbed on to her sister as the dark-hooded hunters formed a circle around Mrs. Bauer. "Come and get me! Come and get me!" Shrieking at the top of her lungs, the woman spun in the white light, arms floating above her head.

And then one of the hunters moved forward quickly. His arms shot up. And in the shifting lights, Destiny saw the wooden stake he held between his hands.

Mrs. Bauer appeared to tumble back as the man lurched forward. He hoisted the stake high over his head—and plunged it into her chest.

Like the howl of a wild animal, Mrs. Bauer's

shrill scream echoed off the trees.

Destiny let go of her sister and covered her ears with her hands. But she couldn't shut out the horrifying wail of anguish.

Then, silence as Mrs. Bauer fell to the grass.

"No! Oh, no." Livvy uttered a low cry.

Destiny gasped and clasped a hand over her sister's mouth.

"Who's that?" a boy called.

A chill of horror rushed down Destiny's back as the hooded figures turned away from the fallen woman.

"There's someone in the woods," a boy said.

"Is that Fletch?" Livvy whispered. "Yes, I think it is."

Destiny and Livvy exchanged a terrified glance.

"More vampires. In the woods. Get them!" one of the men commanded.

The white circles of light turned toward the trees.

Destiny froze as the hunters trotted toward the trees, lights held low, searching the ground.

They're going to catch us and kill us too. They're going to shove a wooden stake in my heart. My own friends. My own friends are going to kill me.

Destiny gave Livvy a shove, and the two girls took off, running side by side, ducking under low branches, dodging shrubs and upraised tree roots.

"This way," a guy shouted, close behind them.

Lights bounced off the tree trunks.

Destiny lowered her head and ran. She darted through a wide patch of tall reeds and kept going. A narrow, trickling creek ran along the other side of the reeds. She and Livvy splashed over the creek, running hard, into the tangle of trees on the other side.

Weird. I'm not breathing hard, Destiny thought. And suddenly, she also realized that she could see the trees and weeds and shrubs so clearly, as if it were daytime.

She saw Livvy shoot ahead, moving from one side to another, darting and dodging as if there were a path.

I've never run this fast, Destiny thought. I can see every tree leaf, every weed, every rock on the ground.

Where are the hunters?

Destiny glanced back. No lights. Their voices far behind.

She and Livvy picked up speed. They were practically flying over the ground now, senses alert, not growing tired, no aches in their sides, not even breathing hard.

"We're okay," Destiny whispered. "We've outrun them."

Livvy murmured, "I never ran so fast."

"Yes, we outran them easily," Destiny replied. "It . . . it's because we're not human anymore. We outran them because we're *creatures* now."

Livvy's mouth dropped open. "You're right, Dee. Something horrible has happened. I can see bats hiding in those trees. And . . . and I can smell their blood. I can hear their blood pulsing, and smell it . . . smell it. . . . Ohh, I feel so sick."

"Oh, Livvy," Destiny wailed and pulled her sister close, into a tight hug. "How much time is left? In a few weeks or a few days, we won't be ourselves anymore. We'll be disgusting night creatures, living for blood, crazy as poor Mrs. Bauer."

"I'm hungry *now*," Livvy moaned.

"We've got to find the Restorer," Destiny said. And then added in a trembling voice, "Soon."

"But how? She didn't give us a clue, Dee."

"I know. She kept saying he was close. Close."

"But that might not be a clue at all. She was out of her mind, Dee. She wasn't making any kind of sense."

"I know, but . . ."

The hunger overcame her so suddenly. A powerful gnawing in her belly, a coiling ache that made her groan.

She saw the raccoons slinking silently at the edge of the woods, gray fur glimmering, tails waving behind them. Destiny counted—six small ones led by a big, fat one.

"Yes! Yes! I'm so hungry!"

Using fallen leaves to wipe the blood from their faces, the girls stepped out of the woods. They found themselves on Steinway Street, five or six blocks from their house.

Destiny checked in all directions. "We lost the hunters," she said, striding toward the street.

"This time," Livvy added glumly. "But what if they saw our car parked there? They'll know—"

"We have to get it—fast."

Deep in thought, they didn't see the figure on the sidewalk until they nearly bumped into him.

Destiny uttered a startled cry.

He wore a dark sweatshirt, his hair flew wildly around his face, and his jeans were stained and torn.

"Ari!" Destiny cried. "What are you doing here?"

Chapter Twenty-Six
Is Ari a Hunter?

"Did you see the hunters?" Ari asked breathlessly. "I heard they were out tonight. I tried to find them."

"We . . . didn't see anyone," Destiny said.

"I'm totally disappointed," Ari said, shaking his head. "I really want to see a vampire."

Does he suspect something? Destiny wondered. How come he's staring at Livvy and me like that?

"Where are you two coming from?" he asked.

They both spoke up at the same time.

"The mall," Livvy said.

"Courtney's house," Destiny answered.

Ari narrowed his eyes at them. "You're putting me on, right?" He stepped up closer to Destiny and pointed. "Is that blood on your chin?"

"Huh?" Destiny gasped and rubbed her chin

with a finger. "Oh, yeah. I just bit my lip. It's nothing."

I don't like the way he's staring at me.

Is Ari lying? Is he actually a vampire hunter? Did he join the hunters? Was he at Coach Bauer's with the others? Did he follow Livvy and me?

I can't believe it. I went over to his house and asked him about everything. I practically *told* him I was a vampire. How could I be so stupid?

"Maybe I'll come by later," Ari said to Destiny.

Come by with your hunter friends? To kill Livvy and me?

"Not a good idea," Destiny said. "Livvy and I have to get our beauty sleep. I mean, school starts tomorrow. Remember school?"

Ari grinned. "Oh, yeah. School. I almost forgot."

"Dee and I have to figure out what we're going to wear," Livvy said. "That could take hours."

"So, Dee, maybe you'll help me with my French this semester?"

Why is he playing this game? Trying to throw us off the track?

"Yeah, sure. No problem," she said.

"Great." He flashed Destiny a smile. "See you guys tomorrow." He pulled the sweatshirt hood over his head, turned, and began to jog toward his house.

Livvy couldn't hide her fear. "Did he see us in the woods just now? Is he one of Coach Bauer's hunters, Dee?"

Destiny shook her head. "I don't know. I don't know what to think."

They returned to the car and drove home in silence. Destiny couldn't stop thinking about Marjory Bauer. Again and again, she heard the woman's shrill scream as the wooden stake came down. She saw the stake pierce the poor woman's body. And then there was such a heavy silence, such a heavy, terrifying silence.

The poor woman wanted to die. She wanted her husband to kill her. Did Coach Bauer finally do it? Was he the hooded figure who drove the stake into her chest?

The twins crept into the house through the back door. "Oh." Destiny uttered a low cry when she heard the voices in the living room. Peeking through the hallway, she saw her dad and Coach Bauer.

Bauer was even more pale than usual. He appeared very upset. He kept burying his face in his hands, then looking up and talking rapidly.

Dr. Weller kept shaking his head sadly.

Both men were speaking just above a whisper. Destiny couldn't make out their words. Frozen in fear, she held on to her sister and stared at the two men.

Is Coach Bauer telling Dad about killing his wife?

Did he see us there in the woods?

The next morning, a raw, gray day threatening rain, Destiny and Livvy gazed at Dark Springs High from across the street.

It was a three-story old-fashioned school building built of yellow bricks that had weathered to a muddy brown over the years. A thick wall of ivy grew up to the slanted, black-slate roof, darkening the front of the school even more. Two tall brick chimneys, side by side at the back of the building, coughed puffs of black smoke into the charcoal sky.

"It looks like some kind of haunted castle today," Livvy said, adjusting her backpack on her shoulders.

"It's just your mood," Destiny said. "And these sunglasses make everything look darker."

The girls' eyes had grown even more sensitive. Now they had to wear sunglasses whenever they went outside.

"How are we going to explain the shades, Dee?"

"Maybe no one will ask."

They crossed the street. Destiny felt a cold drop of rain on her forehead. She and Livvy jogged to the front entrance. They opened the door to the roar of voices and slamming lockers.

Ana-Li stopped Destiny outside the principal's office. "Hey, what's up with the shades?"

"It's some stupid eye infection," Destiny said. "Livvy and I both have it."

Ana-Li turned to look at Livvy across the hall, talking to a group of boys. "Wow. Check out Livvy's low-cut jeans. Are those sexy or what? I can't believe she wore those to school."

Destiny sighed. "Livvy is Livvy."

She caught Ana-Li examining her. "You're so thin, Dee. Are you on a diet or something?"

"Not really."

"Bell's going to ring. You know where your homeroom is?"

"I just got here, Ana-Li. I have to check out the list. Catch you later, okay?"

"Donohue's for lunch? I'll drive."

"Yeah. I guess. Maybe."

Destiny pushed her way through a group of kids to get to the bulletin board where the home-room assignments were listed.

"He's gorgeous," she heard a girl behind her say. "Wait till you see him. I mean, movie-star gorgeous."

"Someone said he's student-teaching for McCall," another girl said. "But I heard he's the new college advisor."

"Maybe he tutors after school," the first girl joked.

Both girls laughed.

Destiny elbowed her way into the crowd around the bulletin board. She found the home-room sheet for seniors and searched for her name.

"Dee, you're in Ms. Downs's room with me."

Destiny turned at the sound of the familiar voice. "Courtney, hi. Hey, you cut your hair."

"Last week," Courtney said, puffing up the sides of her short, bobbed hair. "That ponytail was so lame. Where've you been, Dee? I keep calling you, and—"

"Sorry. Really. Things have been weird."

"Have you been sick? You look kinda pale."

"Well—"

It shows. Everyone can see that I've changed.

"Move it. You're blocking traffic." Fletch gave Destiny a playful shove. "Hey, what's up? I like the shades. Let me see them."

He made a grab for them, but Destiny pulled away. She knew the bright hall lights would burn her eyes.

"Hey, Dee, I only wanted to look at them."

"I've got an eye infection."

"Gross." He backed away, stumbling into some other guys, waving with both hands for her to stay back.

The first bell rang. The hall began to empty out as kids made their way to their homerooms. Destiny looked for Courtney, but she had disappeared down the hall.

Destiny hurried past two boys who looked very lost, obviously freshmen. She hurried up the stairs, her backpack bouncing on her shoulders, then turned to go down the first hall—and walked right into a young man.

"Oh. Sorry."

She stared at him. At his wavy black hair slicked straight back, his broad, tanned forehead, the black, piercing eyes, the warm smile.

He wore a creamy white turtleneck over tight-fitting black slacks. He had a silver stud in one ear.

He must be the gorgeous new teacher. That girl was definitely right!

"Sorry. It was my fault," he said. "I wasn't watching where I was going." He had a slight Italian accent.

"No problem," Destiny managed, a little overcome by his dark-eyed stare, his amazing good looks.

"My name is Lorenzo Angelini," he said. He took her hand and shook it. "But everyone calls me Renz. I'm now here. I truly hope we'll get to know one another."

Part Four

Chapter Twenty-Seven
Lorenzo and Laura

As Renz watched the students hurrying to their classrooms, a familiar longing swept over him. Memories of his youth came flooding back. He pressed his back against the tiled wall, remembering. . . .

If only he could make time go backward. Back to those bright, cloudless days two centuries ago when Laura Hanover walked her father's fields in the tiny farming village of Dark Springs.

Lorenzo Angelini had lived his life in a fog of hunger and desire. For centuries, he knew only hunger—the hunger to remember, the hunger to feed, and the hunger to find the beautiful, lost Laura again.

These desires shaped his life. He had been a vampire for so long, and had consumed so much blood—it had kept him from aging. He appeared young and robust. He could walk in bright daylight without being burned up by the sun.

But daylight was no different than night to him. He lived only to survive the blackness that surrounded him day or night. He lived only to find Laura.

Laura with her creamy skin, her high, proud cheekbones, her sparkling emerald eyes, as green as the high pasture grass they walked through together.

Her voice . . . her wonderful laugh . . .

Renz could no longer hear them. Time had taken them away from him. And now he struggled to hold on to her smile, to remember the sweet gardenia aroma of her perfume. It took all his power to picture her walk, those long strides beneath the skirts that swept over the ground.

That night in the alley in New York, the vampire changed his life forever. Now he lived in eternal winter. Eternal winter . . . until he saw Laura.

A gray fall day. He had been running, fleeing one angry town after another, a stolen, beaver-fur overcoat draped over his tattered black suit.

"What town is this?" he asked the owner of the ramshackle, two-story boardinghouse. Dark

Springs, he was told. Lorenzo took a room for a half dollar a week. At the end of the week, he didn't pay it. He bit the old man's throat instead and drank him dry. The blood was sour, too old, spoiled like a wine gone bad.

That day, he saw Laura. A town market, villagers crowding the narrow Main Street and the open plaza. She was helping her father, carrying a basket of potatoes to a market stand.

Their eyes met.

He stared. She didn't lower her eyes. He felt something—an attraction. Did she feel it too? He couldn't tell by her slow, half smile.

He gathered his courage and walked over to the stand. He knew already that he was in love with her. He knew that he had to win her and keep her with him for all time.

He had to make her immortal too.

She laughed as he teased her about the potatoes. He drew a face on one and said it resembled her father. She grabbed it away from him and protested, "How can I sell it now? Go away. You will make us poor."

But he could tell by the blush on her cheek and the flash of her green eyes that she didn't want him to go away.

Lorenzo knew his charms. So many young women had fallen for him, for his Italian good looks, his wavy dark hair, the mystery in his black eyes. So many young women had fallen . . . and died.

But not Laura, he decided. Laura will live with me through the centuries.

Soon, he was taking long walks with her through the pleasant little village, laughing with her . . . kissing her, gently at first, then showing his passion. What a thrill when she showed the same passion for him!

Seeing his tattered suit and, perhaps, the wild look in his eyes, Laura's father didn't approve of Renz. The couple had to meet secretly in town or at the bubbling springs at the dark rock hills.

One warm summer night by the springs, the scent of marigolds and pine floating in the air, a full moon high in the cloudless sky, Lorenzo wrapped Laura in a tender hug, brought his face close, and whispered, "I want you to be with me always."

To his surprise, she pulled away. "Father will never allow it," she said, tugging tensely at the long sleeves of her blouse. "He is set against you, Renz. For reasons I cannot fathom. He will not allow us to marry, and as much as it tears my heart in two, I cannot go against my father. I have no choice but to follow his wishes."

Lorenzo had expected as much. Farmer Hanover was a big, strong-spirited man, quick to anger. Once, in fury, he had heaved a pitchfork at a traveling salesman and nearly killed the man. And Lorenzo had seen him lift a three-hundred-pound hog off the ground and toss it back into its pen.

The man was a lion with a lovely, gentle doe for a daughter.

Lorenzo gazed up at the yellow full moon as Laura fell back into his arms. Tears rolled down her cheeks and stained the shoulder of his shirt.

"I would wish it any other way," she sobbed, "but we must continue to meet in secret. If Father finds out, there is no telling what he would do. He could kill you, Lorenzo. If his anger got the best of him, he really could."

"I know a way we can be together for always," he whispered. "It will cause a little pain, but only for a short while. And then we will live side by side for eternity."

She gazed at him, her cheeks red and

tearstained, her lovely, green eyes wide, brimming with more tears. "Lorenzo, my darling, what are you saying? I have explained to you that Father will not allow—"

"Your father cannot stop us, Laura," he said. And then he could wait no longer, for the full moon had reached its peak. His curled fangs lowered from his gums. "Ignore the pain, my loved one. After this night, we shall know only pleasure."

He sank his fangs deep into her throat.

She uttered a startled gasp, but made no cry, no scream of protest. She did not fight him or try to squirm free.

Drinking her warm, sweet blood, he knew she was his.

That moment was the happiest of his life.

As he finished, she sank her teeth into his chest and drank his blood.

The bloods mix under a full moon at its peak, he thought. And now Laura is mine.

Blood dripping from their lips, they kissed.

Renz heard the angry, shouting voices, but he didn't want to end the embrace. Hands grabbed him roughly and pulled him away.

Renz turned to see Laura's red-faced father,

chest heaving under his black coat, hands clamped into tight fists. His entire body quivered with rage.

Two somber, bearded men in long waistcoats stood at Farmer Hanover's side. Renz lowered his gaze to the muskets with their long bayonets in their hands.

"Kill him," came Hanover's command.

The men obediently raised their bayonets.

Laura jumped in front of Renz and opened her mouth in a wail of protest. Her father shoved her aside, sent her sprawling to the grass.

Then the two men grabbed Lorenzo by the arms. They held him in place as Hanover raised his giant fist and pounded it into Lorenzo's face.

I can feel pain, Lorenzo realized with surprise.

The fist came down again, this time on Lorenzo's left ear.

He heard Laura scream again.

Another powerful swing and the fist caught him between the eyes. Pain roared through his head.

Groaning, Lorenzo climbed unsteadily to his feet. He jerked free of his two captors, ducked another swipe from her father's tight fist—and took off running into the woods.

Lowering his head into the wind, he dove through the trees. He could hear the thuds of the boots of the men pursuing him. But they could not shift shapes as he could. As he reached the trees, his body shrank into a new form, and he ran as a field mouse, low in the grass.

But his thoughts were not of escape. His thoughts were of Laura.

Her father came too late. He cannot separate us now. He cannot keep us apart. For I have drunk her blood and she has drunk mine, under the light of the full moon.

Lorenzo scampered into a deep hole in the ground. He could hear the men searching for him through the trees, cursing under their breath. He waited for their footsteps to fade.

Laura, I will come to you later tonight. I will come to you after your churlish father has fallen asleep. And I will take you away, take you far from here where you will no longer have to fear him.

He waited until the moon dropped behind the trees. Then, still a field mouse, he made his way through the tall grass of the north pasture, to the back of the low, pine farmhouse.

The field mouse stopped on the sandy

ground behind Laura's bedroom window. Its body raised up, shifted, cracking noisily, the sound of stretching bones, as Lorenzo resumed his human form.

He leaned against the rough wood wall and edged up to the sill of the window. Curtains fluttered in the gentle, warm breeze. The window stood open wide. *As if inviting him in.*

Yes. Laura would be waiting for him. Of course, she would expect him to come rescue her. To come carry her away from this dreary farm forever. To lead her to a life that would transcend the centuries.

He gripped the windowsill and pulled himself up. His boots scraped the pine wall as he let himself inside. The silky curtains tangled around him as he lowered himself to the bedroom floor.

"Laura?" His whisper came out louder than he'd planned, but he heard no reply.

Can she be sleeping so soundly after the terrible scene at the springs?

Lorenzo untangled himself from the curtains and took a step toward her bed. "Laura? I have come for you."

Still no reply.

Her bed came into view against the bare wall. Lingering moonlight cast blue shadows over the folds of the bed quilt.

"Laura?"

He could see her head, tilted slightly on the pillow, her fine, blond hair falling over her face.

Yes. Laura. Beautiful Laura. Waiting for him with her window open.

"Laura? It's me."

He reached out a hand and gently touched the shoulder of her nightdress.

And then he raised his eyes to the bed quilt and saw it . . .

. . . saw it . . .

His eyes bulged and his hand fell off her shoulder.

Howling in rage, in shock, in pain, Lorenzo staggered back, fell back against the curtains. Let them wrap themselves around him again, muffling his screams, his wails of horror and sadness.

Chapter Twenty-Eight
Laura, Again

Through the gauzy curtains, he could see it silhouetted in the faint, dying moonlight.

The stake.

A wooden stake, driven through Laura's chest. A circle of dark blood, dried now, around the stake, running onto the quilt.

Laura. Beautiful Laura, sleeping so peacefully, arms under the quilt, hair sliding over her lovely, pale face.

Laura, murdered by her own father, murdered to keep her from Lorenzo, from the eternal life he had planned for them together.

Lorenzo pulled the curtains around him as if forming a cocoon—a cocoon to hide him from the sight of his beautiful Laura, lying so peacefully in her bed, the wooden stake protruding up from her still body, tilting toward the wall.

Another sob escaped his throat. He wrapped the curtains tighter around him and shut his eyes. But that didn't stop the tears from falling.

And then his grief turned to fury. He ripped the curtains away, planted a final kiss on Laura's cold cheek. Then he made his way to her father's room.

The man was awake, sitting in a wooden rocking chair beside a dying fire. His features were twisted in anger. Large drops of sweat glistened on his forehead.

His big, powerful hands gripped something in his lap. Only his eyes moved when Lorenzo entered the room.

He's waiting for me, Lorenzo thought.

In the flickering red light from the remaining embers, he saw the object in Hanover's hands—a pointed fence post.

He plans to kill me too. But no. Laura will be avenged.

Lorenzo dove for Hanover's throat and sliced into it with his fangs. Hanover opened his mouth to protest, but only a gurgling sound escaped.

The wooden stake fell from his hands and clattered onto the floor.

Lorenzo drank his fill, drained the man,

then ripped open his throat with his hands. He wrenched Hanover's head off, and flung it into the fire.

His heart still pounding with fury, he took one last look at the goggle-eyed head lying upside down in the orange embers. Then he left, lowering himself from the window, into the darkness.

Darkness for the decades to come. How many years passed? Nearly two hundred? He couldn't remember.

He couldn't bear to venture very far from Dark Springs. He kept to himself, prowling at night for creatures on which to feed. The decades passed without hope, without pleasure of any kind, without light.

Until he saw Laura again.

Laura?

No! It couldn't be!

But she had Laura's face, her high cheekbones, her smile, her bright green eyes. Lorenzo stared at her, frozen in disbelief. Stared at her across the high school parking lot.

She leaned against a black SUV, her eyes on the back entrance, tapping the car roof impatiently with one hand. Her fine, blond hair fell loosely to her collar. Her face . . .

Her face . . .

Laura.

She checked her watch. He saw the wedding ring on her finger. She brushed back her hair. She bit her lip fretfully.

Lorenzo's excitement, his disbelief, held him back. But he forced himself to approach her. "Have we met? I believe I know you." He flashed her his most charming smile.

Still biting her lip, she narrowed her eyes at him. "No. I don't think so."

Lorenzo scratched his head. "I'm so sorry. My mistake. I knew a woman named . . . Hanover. She resembled you so much, I—"

"Hanover?" the woman's eyes grew wide. "Really? There were some Hanovers in my family. But that was way back, generations ago."

He grinned. "I see. I must be confused. I'm Lorenzo Angelini," he told her. "Are you waiting for someone?"

She turned back to the school. "Yes, my daughters. I told them I'd pick them up now. I should go in and get them." She saw his outstretched hand. "Oh. Sorry. I'm Deborah

Weller. Nice to meet you."

The touch of her hand thrilled him. He held on to it until she pulled it away.

The back door of the high school opened. Two blond-haired girls came running out.

"Destiny! Livvy! Over here," Deborah called.

She motioned to her daughters to hurry, and pulled open the car door. "Nice to meet you, Mr. Angelini."

"Nice to meet you too."

Very nice indeed.

Chapter Twenty-Nine
The Vampire's Kiss

"Who has the cheese fries?"

Ari raised his hand and the waitress dropped the plate in front of him next to his double cheeseburger.

"You on a diet, Ari?" Ana-Li reached across the table and grabbed a cheese fry off the plate. "Ow. They're hot."

Ari grinned at her. "Take another one and I'll smack you."

Ana-Li grabbed another one.

Ari grabbed her wrist. "Drop. Drop."

Destiny saw the manager watching them. "Give it a rest, guys. How embarrassing would it be to get kicked out of Donohue's?"

"It wouldn't be the first time," Ari said. He bent Ana-Li's wrist back until she dropped the fry—into his Coke. Ana-Li burst out laughing.

Livvy appeared beside the booth. She gave

Ari a shove. "Move it over." She squeezed in next to him. "You already ordered?" She gazed at Destiny's plate. "Two hamburgers?"

Destiny nodded. "I'm starving."

"You never used to eat burgers rare like that," Ana-Li said. "Yuck. It looks like blood dripping from them."

Livvy waved the waitress over. "I'll have a hamburger too. Very, very rare, and a diet Coke." She turned to Ana-Li. "What's up?"

"Ari won't share his fries."

Ari slammed his hands on the table. "Here. Take them all." He shoved the plate toward Ana-Li.

"Thanks." Ana-Li began eating them one by one.

Livvy leaned across the table and whispered. "Hear what the girls in the next booth are talking about? That new guidance counselor. What's-his-name? Renz."

Ari grinned. "Yeah. He's always telling everyone to call him Renz. What kinda name is that? Sounds like something from a sci-fi movie. Renz the Destroyer!"

"He is definitely cute," Ana-Li said.

Destiny put down her fork. "Cute? You're

kidding, right? He's not cute. He's totally gorgeous."

Ana-Li giggled. "Dee likes the dark, mysterious types."

"Hey, I have an appointment with him after school," Destiny said. Across the table, Livvy had a scowl on her face. "Liv, what's your problem?"

Livvy shook her head and sighed. "Nothing. No big thing. Really. Well . . ."

"What is it?" Destiny asked.

Livvy played with one long, dangling earring. "Just thinking about Bree. You know. How she's missing senior year and everything."

"I miss her too," Ana-Li said in a whisper.

Ari swallowed a big chunk of cheeseburger. "On TV this morning, they said the police don't have a clue about the Vampire Killer. And the hunters don't have a clue either."

Destiny gaped at him. "The hunters? What about the hunters? They were on TV?"

Ari's cheeks burned red. "No. Some guys were talking. You know. About vampires in town and the vampire hunters. I really don't know much about it. You've heard the rumors too—right?"

He took another bite of cheeseburger,

avoiding Destiny's eyes.

So he really is one of the hunters, Destiny decided. Why did he blush like that? Because he didn't mean to mention them. It just slipped out.

Destiny gazed across the table at Ari and felt a shiver race down her back. I've known Ari since third grade. Is he really going to hunt me down and kill me? Are Livvy and I really going to be killed by our own friends?

"Bree would have loved the senior overnight trip," Livvy said. "She was really looking forward to it."

"Yes, she would have," Ari said, sighing. His expression brightened. "I'm bringing a super-sized sleeping bag. You know. In case any girls get lonely during the night." He grinned at Destiny.

"Some kids got caught last year," Ana-Li said. "Mr. Arthur walked into the tent and . . . there they were, messing around. It was so not cool."

"I heard about it," Livvy said. "They both got suspended."

"Worth it," Ari said, cheeseburger grease running down his chin. He grinned at Destiny. Destiny looked away.

Ana-Li handed him a napkin. "I heard the school is bringing a lot more chaperones this year," she said. "You know. To make sure no one messes around."

"Hey, maybe Renz will be a chaperone." Destiny tried to join the conversation.

"You've really got a thing for him," Livvy said, frowning at her sister.

Destiny shrugged. "What's your problem? I can't like older guys?"

"Anyway, the senior overnight should be cool if it doesn't rain," Ana-Li said. "I heard it's a four-mile hike to get to the camping ground."

"Can't we drive?" Ari asked. He laughed at his own joke. "Guess what? It's gonna be a full moon that night." He grinned at Ana-Li and did a werewolf howl. "Owooooo. It could get pretty freaky."

Destiny shuddered. She hadn't known it was the night of the full moon. She suddenly felt cold all over.

Livvy glanced at her watch. "Where's Ross? He said he'd meet me."

"Are you sure?" Destiny asked. "He's been at that booth behind you for half an hour. He's with Courtney." She pointed.

"Huh? You're joking." Livvy spun around.

Ross sat beside Courtney in the booth near the front. He had his arm draped around her shoulders, and their faces were close together as they talked. They both laughed and Courtney pressed her forehead against his cheek.

Livvy jumped to her feet. "I don't believe it. That creep. What's he doing with Courtney?"

She stepped away from the booth and went storming down the aisle.

"Livvy—come back," Destiny called. "Hey— just calm down. What are you going to do?"

Her hair bouncing behind her, Livvy strode past Ross's booth. She kept her eyes straight ahead. She totally ignored them. Destiny watched her bang the glass front door open and disappear outside.

"Whoa. Bad news." Ana-Li clapped a hand over her mouth.

The waitress appeared with Livvy's hamburger and drink. She stared at the empty spot in the booth. "Is she coming back?"

"I don't think so," Destiny said.

After school, Destiny made her way down the stairs, past the empty lunchroom, and found

Renz's office at the end of the hall next to a janitor's closet. She knocked on the wooden door, then pushed it open.

She saw him standing at an empty bookcase, his back to her. He turned as she entered, and a smile crossed his face.

His wavy hair glistened under the single ceiling light. His dark eyes flashed. "Welcome to my castle." He motioned around the room.

"I think it used to be a supply closet," Destiny said. The narrow room had no windows. The bookcase, a low file cabinet, a desk, a desk chair, and a folding chair in front of the desk were the only furnishings.

"You know the old joke," he said. "The room is so small, I have to go outside to change my mind."

Destiny laughed, harder than she meant to.

He motioned for her to sit down in the folding chair.

She gazed at the empty shelves. "Mr. Angelini, where's all your stuff?"

He lowered himself to the edge of the desk in front of her. She could smell his aftershave or cologne, sharp, not sweet. "Please. Renz," he said, leaning over her. "My books haven't arrived yet. They were delayed. I feel so lost without them." He smiled at her again, his black eyes locked on hers.

Destiny felt a shiver of excitement.

"I need to decorate," he said. "Put something up on the wall. Something colorful." He sighed. "I'm not good at transitions. Moving to a new town. A new job. It takes me a while to get going."

Destiny smiled up at him. "I don't know what it's like. I've lived in Dark Springs my whole life."

I feel so comfortable with him. It's strange. As if I've known him a long time. This is our first conversation, but I'm not nervous at all.

He stood up and closed the door. "We should talk about colleges. I'll get your file, Laura."

Destiny blinked. "Laura? No. I'm Destiny."

He stood close. The aroma of the cologne washed over her. She inhaled a piney smell, an outdoors smell, the smell of the woods.

"No," he whispered, "you're Laura. Don't you remember me, Laura? Aren't you happy to see me again?"

With surprising strength, he pulled her to her feet.

"Mr. Angelini, please. I don't understand. I—"

Destiny made no attempt to resist as he
wrapped her in his arms, brought her face up to
his, and pressed his lips to hers.

Chapter Thirty
Destiny Finds the Restorer

"Laura . . . Laura . . ." he whispered when the kiss finally ended.

Destiny gazed into his eyes. I know you. I know your thoughts. I know who you are.

The room darkened, as if a gray fog had risen over them. The piney aroma carried her to the woods. In the darkening fog, she could hear the flutter of birds' wings, the cry of night animals, and the rasping chirp of crickets.

"You remember me, don't you, Laura?" he whispered, his breath tingling her ear. The tingle continued down her neck, her back. She knew she was shivering. She couldn't stop.

He held her tightly. "You remember me. And you remember our love for each other. You remember the full moon . . . the night our love changed us, blood for blood."

His gaze didn't move from her eyes. He didn't blink.

Destiny felt powerless to look away, to move, to protest. She took a deep breath and finally found her voice. "You have powers . . ." Her words came out muffled, as if from far away.

Renz gazed at her. "What did you say?"

"You're doing something to me. You have powers, don't you?"

A smile spread slowly over his face. "Well . . ."

"Please tell me. Tell me about your powers."

A jarring sound made her jump.

A knock on the door.

Renz let go of her and moved back.

The door swung open. The fog lifted.

Blinking, Destiny stared at Ari as he poked his head into the room.

His eyes went wide. "Oh. Sorry." He didn't let go of the doorknob. "I didn't know you were busy, Renz." He squinted at Destiny. "How's it going, Dee?"

She blinked. "Fine."

"Did he get you into college yet?" Ari asked.

Renz chuckled. "In case you don't realize it, Ari, getting into college is a long process." He edged away from Destiny and stepped up to Ari. "Did you want me for something?"

"You said you had brochures. You know, from Brown and Tufts."

"Let me see." Frowning, Renz moved to his file cabinet and began sifting through the top drawer.

Destiny gazed at him, so good-looking in that black turtleneck, those tight, black jeans.

Renz handed Ari a couple of brightly colored brochures. "I'm not sure if they accept the standard application," Renz said, backing Ari to the door. "I'll check."

Destiny climbed unsteadily to her feet. "I guess we're finished for today?"

Renz turned and stared at her. He appeared to be thinking hard. "Yes, we're done." His smile made her feel so warm. "But we need to talk about school visits. Discuss it with your parents, okay? Then we'll talk again."

Destiny thanked him and made her way out of the tiny closet. Ari was waiting for her in the hall. "How'd it go, Dee?"

"Okay, I guess."

They walked together past the lunchroom, then up the stairs. "Are you in love with him like all the other girls in the senior class?"

Destiny laughed. "He's pretty damn cute."

Ari shook his head. "Aren't college advisors supposed to have all kinds of books and papers and stuff? His office is totally empty. He spends all his time out in the hall, flirting with every girl who passes by."

"Ooh, jealous, jealous," Destiny teased.

"Oh, for sure," he replied, but his cheeks turned bright pink.

"Ari, how come you're here so late after school?"

He shrugged. "I had a few things to do. You walking home?"

"No, I drove this morning. Want a lift?"

"Hey, yeah. Good deal. Thanks."

She drove him to his house. They talked about French class. He made her promise to help him. They gossiped about some kids who'd been cutting class to hang out in their cars at the springs. Ari talked about two new horror DVDs he'd rented, both of which he said were awesome.

Destiny pretended to listen, but she barely heard a word Ari said. She still felt strange, off-balance, fogged in. She couldn't stop thinking about Renz.

He was so warm, so friendly and caring. Some of their conversation drifted back to her.

Just words and phrases, floating in her mind . . .
Blood for blood . . . powers . . . full moon . . .
Laura . . .

Destiny struggled to make sense of it all.

Suddenly, she realized that Ari was staring at her. At the marks on her throat? Was he staring at the marks on her throat and figuring out what had happened to her?

"Dee, there's something I have to tell you," he said softly.

She pulled the car into his driveway. Her heart started to pound. She couldn't speak. She nodded, signaling him to go on.

"Well . . ." He hesitated. His hands fidgeted at his sides. "It's just that . . . I . . . kinda like you."

Then he lurched toward her and pressed his lips against hers.

The kiss lasted only a few seconds. Destiny was so shocked, she barely kissed him back.

He grinned at her. "Maybe I'll see you later."

"Yeah, maybe," she replied, still stunned.

He jumped out of the car.

Destiny drove home, pulled the car into the garage, and hurried straight up to her room. "Hey, Liv," she called.

Livvy sat at the computer, typing an e-mail.

She finished her note, sent it, then turned to face Destiny. "Where've you been?"

Destiny tossed her backpack onto the floor. "I told you. I had an appointment with Mr. Angelini."

"How'd it go?" Before Destiny could answer, Livvy said, "Oh, by the way, while I was online, you got an IM from Nakeisha."

Destiny walked over to her sister. "Yeah? What'd she say?"

"She's coming to Dark Springs. On Saturday. She's doing college visits in Boston. But she said her mother would drop her off here for an hour or two."

"Cool."

But Destiny wasn't thinking about Nakeisha.

"What did you and Renz talk about?" Livvy asked. "My appointment isn't until after the senior overnight."

"We . . . well, we talked about . . ." Destiny struggled to remember. Struggled to put the words together.

"He . . . he said something about blood," she said, thinking hard.

Livvy had been adjusting her nose stud. Her

features widened in shock. "He—what?"

"Oh my God," Destiny murmured. "Oh my God, Liv. He talked about blood. Yes. I can remember it now. He said something about blood for blood, about the full moon."

Destiny shook her head, as if trying to shake the words out, as if trying to tug out a clear memory.

Livvy stood up and stared at her sister, her head tilted, her expression alarmed. "Dee, are you okay? Are you cracking up?"

"Oh my God. Oh my God," Destiny repeated, still shaking her head. "It's true, Liv. I . . . I asked him if he had powers. And he said *yes*!"

"But, Dee—"

"Oh my God. Don't you see, Liv? Don't you see?"

Livvy narrowed her eyes at Destiny. "See what?"

"Renz is the one," Destiny said, her voice breaking with emotion. "He was letting me know today. Renz is the one, see? *Renz is the Restorer!*"

Chapter Thirty-One
Livvy vs. Courtney

*S*unday night, the girls retreated to their room. Destiny had an essay due for French class, but she sat staring at her computer, unable to get Renz out of her mind.

Tomorrow morning, we'll see him first thing. We'll ask him to restore us, to give us back our normal lives. He can help us. I know he can. Livvy and I are going to be okay.

Across the room, Livvy talked on the phone to friends.

Loud voices interrupted them. Destiny turned to see Ross and Ari at the top of the stairs.

"What's up? Last-minute homework?" Ari asked.

"Did you hear about Charley Robbins?" Ross asked. "He was caught stealing doughnuts from the Pick 'N Pay. You believe it? He had a box of doughnuts under his sweatshirt. What a total jerk."

"He's toast. He's dead meat," Ari said. "Someone said he did it on a dare."

"I ran six miles this afternoon," Ross said. "All along the reservoir. It was great. I'm in shape for basketball, I think. Fletch was supposed to meet me, but he never showed up. I called him, and he said he has turf toe. How can you have turf toe if you've never been on turf?"

Ari rubbed his stomach. "You got anything to eat? My parents were out, and I forgot to have dinner."

Normal life, Destiny thought. After Livvy and I see Renz, we'll go back to a normal life. We won't have to worry every time the doorbell rings. We won't have to wonder if Ross and Ari are vampire hunters.

She ran down to the kitchen to make Ari a sandwich. To her surprise, he followed her. "I didn't really want a sandwich," he said. "I thought maybe we could be alone." He kissed her again, this time longer.

She pulled away. "Ari, I—don't know what to say. I mean, I'm not sure . . ."

He sighed. "Maybe I *will* have that sandwich."

She made a ham sandwich for him. Then

they returned to the room upstairs.

Destiny instantly saw that Livvy and Ross had made up. They were pressed together on the couch. Livvy had one leg over his lap, and her arms were around him. Her hair fell over his face as she kissed him.

Footsteps on the stairs. Courtney appeared.

She had a blue knit cap over her brown hair. She wore a pale blue sweater over a red T-shirt and khaki cargo pants. "Hey, what's up, Dee?"

Her smile faded when she saw Livvy and Ross across the room.

Livvy swiveled around, but she still had one leg over Ross's lap. Her red lipstick was smeared around her mouth.

"Ross, you creep!" Courtney cried through gritted teeth. She stomped over to the couch. "You said you were coming to my house!"

Ross raised both hands, signaling for a truce. He tried to disentangle himself from Livvy. But she slid an arm around his shoulders and snuggled close, staring up at Courtney, challenging her.

"Guess he forgot," Livvy said, smoothing back Ross's blond hair.

"You *bitch*!" Courtney screamed. She dove

at Livvy, grabbed her by the shoulders, struggled to pull her to her feet.

"Let go of me," Livvy said.

"Hey, let me up!" Ross pushed Livvy out of the way and stood up, dancing away from the couch. "Courtney—stop!"

Sobbing, Courtney tugged Livvy up. She gripped Livvy's hair with both hands and pulled.

Livvy let out an angry cry. She ducked her head, but couldn't free herself from Courtney's grip. "Let go! Let go of me!"

"Hey, stop it! Both of you! Stop it!" Destiny screamed.

But both girls ignored her. Courtney jerked Livvy's head from side to side. The two girls wrestled on their feet.

Livvy grabbed Courtney's arm. She snapped it hard.

Destiny heard a sickening *crack*.

Livvy let go of her and stepped back, breathing hard, eyes wide with surprise.

Courtney's arm dropped limply to her side. Screaming, she fell to her knees. "You broke it! You broke my arm!"

Livvy turned to Destiny. "I didn't mean

to. It just snapped!"

"It hurts! It hurts!" Courtney moaned. She struggled to raise her arm, and let out a cry of pain.

Destiny hurried over to her. Ross helped Courtney to stand.

"It was an accident," Livvy said, pressing her hands to the sides of her face. "Really. I hardly did anything."

Courtney cradled the broken arm in her good arm. "I can't stand it. It hurts so much."

Destiny felt her stomach lurch when she saw ragged bone poking out through the torn skin. "We've got to get her to the hospital." She turned to Ari. "Did you drive?"

"I'll take her," Ross said. He helped Courtney to the stairs.

Tears poured down Courtney's cheeks. She turned and scowled at Livvy. "You jealous bitch. You've snapped it in two! How could you do this to me? I'll kill you for this!"

Livvy opened her mouth to protest, but no sound came out.

Ross slid his arm around Courtney's shoulders and guided her down the stairs.

"Ross, don't go!" Livvy called. "Stay with

me. Let Ari take her."

Ross didn't answer. Ari hurried to the stairs. "I'd better go with them and help out."

They disappeared down the stairs. Destiny heard the kitchen door slam behind them.

Livvy hugged herself. She crossed the room to Destiny. "I hardly touched her," she said. "It was just an accident. I didn't try to break her arm. You believe me, right?"

Destiny sighed. "Yes, I believe you."

Livvy shut her eyes. "Courtney started it. She grabbed me first. What does she think she's doing? She knows I love Ross."

Destiny gasped. "Love? Did you say 'love'?"

Livvy nodded. She opened her eyes. "Yes, I did. Why are you staring at me?"

"Well . . . for one thing, Ross is probably a vampire hunter. Do you think he'd love you back if he knew—"

"He cares for me. He told me so."

"But you know Ross. He never goes with anyone for long. He always has three or four girls chasing him."

"This is different," Livvy insisted. "He and I—we've talked. He's serious about me. Courtney has been trying to break us up. But I can't let her do that. She asked for it, Dee. She really did."

Destiny shook her head. "She asked for it? She asked for a broken arm? Did you see the bone sticking out through the skin?"

"I'd like to do worse to her."

"Don't say that, Livvy. That's horrible."

A sob escaped Livvy's throat. "You don't understand me, Dee. You're just like everyone else."

"Stop talking like that," Destiny snapped. "We have more important things—"

"Nothing is more important than Ross and me!" Livvy screamed.

"Calm down. Calm down. You're not thinking clearly. Listen to me, Liv. Right now, getting to Renz is more important. We have to see him as soon as we can and tell him we need his special powers. We—"

Destiny stopped when she heard the front door slam. A few seconds later, she heard heavy, trudging footsteps in the kitchen.

Both girls went to the stairs. "Dad, is that you? Are you home?" Destiny called.

No answer.

Destiny led the way down the stairs. "Dad?"

He had his back to them. He was hunched over the sink, washing his hands.

"Dad?"

When he turned, Destiny let out a cry. His shirt was torn open and stained. Streams of dark blood had caked on his forehead. Both hands were cut and bleeding.

"Oh my God!" Destiny cried. "Dad—are you okay? What happened?"

Chapter Thirty-Two
"Her Blood Was Drained"

"I'm okay," he said. "Really."

"But, Dad—"

Both girls rushed over to him. "What happened?" Destiny repeated.

"A little car accident," he said.

Livvy caught him as his knees started to fold. "A car accident? Are you hurt? Are you okay?"

"I'm fine, really." He swung free of Livvy and stuck his hands under the rushing hot water in the sink. "My mind wandered, I guess. I hit a mailbox. No big deal."

Destiny stared at him. "Your mind wandered? Dad, you've got to get yourself together. You could have been killed."

"I know," he said, shaking his head. "But I'm fine. Really."

"You're not fine," Destiny said. "You're not yourself, and you know it."

"You've been working too hard," Livvy said. "Look what time it is."

"I know. I know," he muttered. "When you're right, you're right." He forced a smile. Then he shut off the water and went dripping across the kitchen, heading to his room.

Destiny and Livvy exchanged nervous glances. "He's all cut up," Livvy murmured.

"I'm really worried about him," Destiny said.

She looked out the kitchen window. Her dad's SUV stood in the driveway, close to the garage. Light from the kitchen washed over it.

"That's so weird," she said to Livvy. "Come here. Check this out. Dad's car . . . it looks perfectly fine."

Two days later, the phone woke her up. Destiny raised her head off the pillow and gazed out the window. The morning sky was still charcoal gray.

She fumbled for the phone and picked it up. "Hello?" Her voice was still hoarse from sleep.

She heard someone crying on the other end. "Hello? Who is this?"

Muffled sobs. Then a choked voice she

didn't recognize. "Dee, it's me."

"Who? Please—"

"I'm sorry. I can't stop crying."

"Ana-Li? Is that you? What's wrong? Are you okay?"

"Yes, I'm okay. I mean, no. You see, Courtney . . . it's Courtney . . ."

A shock jolted Destiny wide awake. She jerked up in bed and dropped her feet to the floor. "Courtney? Yes, I know. She broke her arm the other night."

"Her arm? No. No. No. She's dead, Dee," Ana-Li said between sobs. "Her parents . . . they found her in the backyard. She's dead. Her blood . . . oh my God . . . her blood was drained, Dee. Courtney's dead."

Destiny held a hand over her mouth to keep from screaming. Ana-Li's voice sounded unreal in her ears. The words weren't making sense.

She didn't *want* the words to make sense.

Please let this be a mistake.

But no. Through her sobs, Ana-Li continued. "There's no school. School is canceled. Everyone is afraid. It's so frightening, Dee. The Vampire Killer—he . . . he struck again. Poor Courtney. I . . . can't believe it. I just saw her yesterday. First Bree and now . . ."

The Vampire Killer?

No. I don't think so.

"I . . . I'll call you back, Ana-Li. I can't talk now. Later, okay? I . . . I'm too upset." She clicked off the phone and tossed it onto the bed.

"Livvy!" she screamed.

She stared at her sister across the room, on her stomach, hair spilling over the pillow, one hand trailing over the side of the bed to the floor.

"Livvy—you killed her!"

Livvy raised her head sleepily. "What are you talking about?"

"Don't pretend. Don't play innocent with me." Destiny grabbed her twin by the shoulders and shook her awake. "You killed her. You killed Courtney."

Livvy pushed Destiny's hands away and yawned. "Oh my God! Courtney's dead?" She shut her eyes. "How? How did it happen?"

"You know how!" Destiny cried. "You did it—didn't you, Livvy! You were afraid you'd lose Ross. So you—you—" Destiny's voice broke into sobs.

Livvy turned her face away from Destiny.

"That's horrible," she murmured. "Horrible news. I really can't believe it."

Trembling, Destiny stared down at her sister. "You're not even pretending to be sorry. How *could* you, Livvy? Courtney didn't have to die—just because she and Ross—"

"Leave Ross out of it," Livvy snapped. "I didn't do it, Dee. I swear to you."

Destiny's voice broke again. "My own sister. I . . . I can't even *look* at you."

"Well, you won't have to for long."

"What does *that* mean?" Destiny cried. "What are you saying? Have you gone crazy? Are you that far gone? Have you gone nuts like Mrs. Bauer?"

"Speak for yourself, Dee." Livvy stood up and, pulling down her nightshirt, made her way to the bathroom.

Destiny strode up behind her and spun her around. "Livvy—you killed for Ross. You killed a human being. Doesn't that mean anything to you? Don't you even realize what's happened to you? Don't you think about the trouble we're both in? We have to find Renz right away. We have to be restored."

"Maybe I have my own plan," Livvy said

through gritted teeth.

"Huh? What are you saying?"

Livvy dove into the bathroom and slammed the door.

"What are you saying, Livvy?" Destiny demanded. "What kind of plan?"

Chapter Thirty-Three
A Valuable Nature Lesson

"Where's your sister?" Ana-Li asked.

Destiny shrugged. "Beats me. She left the house right after breakfast. She didn't say a word to me."

"She's just afraid," Ana-Li said. "We all are. Our friends are dying off one by one. None of us knows how to deal with it. So Livvy acts angry. That's her way. She'll calm down . . . once they catch the murderer."

Destiny spent the day at Ana-Li's house. Ari and Fletch and some other kids dropped by after lunch. No one felt much like talking. But somehow it felt safer to be together.

Destiny thought about Livvy all day. And she thought about Renz. *School is closed. Livvy and I can't see him today. How much longer can we wait?*

She returned home at dinnertime to find the house empty. A phone message from Dad said that he was working late and that Mikey was staying at a friend's. No sign of Livvy.

Destiny didn't feel hungry, but she shoved a frozen pizza into the oven. She forced down a slice without even tasting it, then went up to her room. She began to pace back and forth, wondering what she should do next.

She picked up Livvy's nightshirt from where it had been tossed on the floor, folded it, and placed it on Livvy's bed. Livvy's eye shadows and lipsticks were a jumble on her dressing table. Destiny began to straighten them, putting caps on the tubes and bottles.

Destiny didn't start to feel strange until just after eight o'clock. That's when her skin started to tingle, her back itched, and she felt a powerful gnawing sensation in the pit of her stomach.

She ignored it at first. But the tingling became an ache and the gnawing, tumbling feeling in her stomach nearly doubled her over.

I need some fresh air.

She opened the window and took several deep breaths. She gripped the windowsill so tightly her hands ached.

Please . . . please . . . make this stop.

So hungry. I'm so hungry.

She felt her hair stiffen and heard it crackle. And then her skin was crackling too. Her grip on the sill loosened, and her hands shrank quickly.

What's happening to me?

She felt herself pulling inward . . . closing in . . . changing so fast. All crackly and stiff.

Muscles tightened. Vision blurred. Banging heartbeats made her chest throb.

Am I sick? What's happening? I can't control it!

She saw her clothes in a rumpled pile below her. She felt herself floating up, floating effortlessly.

She fluttered off the windowsill. Sailed across the room, up to her dresser mirror.

"NOOOOOOOO!" Her scream escaped as a shrill whistle.

Spreading her wings, she squinted into the mirror. Her sight strange, fragmented. But she could see clearly enough.

She could see her fur-covered body attached to the thin, veined wings, her tiny, red eyes, her rodent mouth hanging open as she stared . . .

. . . stared at the bat in the mirror.

Screeching in horror, she turned, flapping

her wings frantically, and spun in midair.

Hungry. So hungry now.

She sailed through the open window, out into the night.

I'm not human anymore. I'm a bat. I . . . want to go home. I want to go back.

But the hunger drove her through the purple-gray sky, over the dark houses. The cool wind felt good, rushing under her wings. She could feel her rapid heartbeats drumming in her chest, and feel the gnawing hunger in her belly.

Her wings flapped silently as she swooped low over a wooded field—and found what she was searching for. An owl on a high tree limb, staring straight ahead, so still, feathers bristling in the wind. A fat owl, filled with delicious blood . . .

She swooped at it, opening her mouth hungrily. Screeching down, she dug her teeth into its chest.

She didn't expect it to fight back. But the owl slashed a deep cut in her left wing. Thrashing wildly, it tore at her belly with its beak.

They tumbled off the tree branch. Fell to the mossy, wet ground.

The owl thrashed and cut. Destiny flapped hard above it, keeping her long teeth clamped deep in its belly.

The owl screeched, clawing at her wings, thrusting its beak into her middle, sharp jab after jab.

Pain shot through Destiny's body, paralyzing her. She lost her grip on its belly. Blood spattered her throbbing body, and she realized it was her own blood.

I've made a horrible mistake. I didn't know . . . owls are stronger . . . stronger than bats. I didn't know . . .

Too weak to flap her wings . . . too weak to escape.

She lay on her back on the blood-wet grass, the owl perched on her tiny, gray belly. Its talons tore at her thin wings again. Its beak dug into her throat.

I didn't know . . . I didn't know . . .

Chapter Thirty-Four
A Surprise From Dad

Destiny opened her eyes.

I can't see. I'm blind.

But then the stars came into focus. And the nearly full moon behind wisps of gray cloud.

She saw the roof of her garage. Raised her head from the grass, turned, and saw the back of her house.

I'm lying in the grass behind my house. I'm totally naked.

She sat up. Rubbed her chest. Dried blood.

It's real. It really happened.

How did I fight off the owl? How am I still alive?

Slowly, the terrifying memory came back. As the owl attacked her, she had started to transform. Back to her human body, hands furiously shoving the bird away.

The startled owl raised its wings, turned, and flew off into the night.

Destiny shivered. Her legs were wet with dew, so cold against her skin. She pulled a brown leaf from her hair, then got up onto her knees.

She turned to the house. Mikey's yellow bike stood propped against the back wall next to his soccer ball. She could see lights on in the kitchen and in the room above the garage—her room.

She stood up slowly, testing her arms and legs. Her muscles ached, but she could walk. Keeping in the darkest shadows, she made her way to the back door and peered in.

No one in the kitchen.

Silently, she pried open the door and slipped inside. The clock over the stove read eight forty-five. She had been gone less than an hour. She listened for voices. No. No music, no TV on. No one home yet.

Still shivering, her mind spinning, Destiny crept up to her room. She took a long shower. And as the steamy hot water rushed over her, she decided.

I have to tell Dad.

I can't keep this a secret anymore. It's gone too far. I turned into a bat tonight. What if it's too late for me? What if it's too late for Renz to fix me?

I'm too scared to face it all alone. I'm no longer in control of my own body. The moon is nearly full. I have to tell Dad. I can't keep it all inside me any longer.

She pulled on a T-shirt, an oversized sweater, and jeans, grabbed the car keys, and hurried out to the garage. Dad had the SUV, but the Civic was still in its place.

Destiny's hands shook. She grabbed the steering wheel to steady them.

I have to tell Dad. After all, he is a doctor. Maybe . . . maybe . . .

She backed the car out, nearly scraping the driver's side against the garage wall.

Calm down, Dee. Concentrate on your driving.

She glanced at the dashboard clock. Nearly nine thirty and Dad was still at work. That poor man. Why is he working so hard?

The streets slid by in a blur. Before she realized it, she was pulling to the curb in front of her dad's animal clinic. Street lights washed over the square, redbrick building. The sign above the glass door was simple, stenciled in blue letters on white: WELLER VETERINARY CLINIC.

Destiny climbed out of the car. She wiped her cold, wet hands on the legs of her jeans. Her heart thudded in her chest.

I've never been so nervous to talk to Dad. What will he think when I tell him? What will he say?

The blinds were only half closed on the wide front window beside the entrance, and she could see that the lights were on in her dad's waiting room. The examining rooms and the lab were at the back.

Destiny took a deep breath and made her way to the door. But a flash of movement in the window caught her attention. She turned and stepped to the window, stooping to see inside between the blinds.

"Oh, wow."

She slid to the side so she wouldn't be seen. Her dad sat on the waiting room desk, gesturing and talking to a group of guys seated in front of him.

They had their backs to the window. Keeping out of view, Destiny squinted hard into the brightly lit room.

It's some kind of meeting. But that doesn't

make sense. Why would Dad be having a meeting this time of night?

And then she recognized Ross in the chair closest to the window. And Fletch beside him. And across the room, other guys from Dark Springs High.

Destiny slid away from the window. She pressed her back against the cold brick wall.

What are those guys doing there with my dad?

What could they be talking about?

Holding on to the brick wall, she leaned forward again and peered into the window. They were all standing up. She could hear the scrape of their chairs. Her father opened the coat closet door. He leaned inside.

A car passed behind her on the street, sending its headlights over Destiny. She stood up straight. The car slowed, then continued on its way.

Her eyes burned from the bright lights. Blinking hard, she swung back to the window. Dr. Weller stepped out of the coat closet. Destiny could see him clearly. She could see what he was holding. Wooden stakes, sharpened to a point at one end. He handed one to each boy.

"Oh, no."

She didn't want to believe what she was seeing. Staring through the window glass was like staring into a dream.

That isn't my dad. Those aren't my friends.

She didn't have long to think about it. Someone shut off the lights in the waiting room. The window went black.

They're coming out.

Chapter Thirty-Five
Is Ross Dangerous?

I don't believe it. But it's true. Dad is a hunter—Dad and my friends are vampire hunters.

Destiny spun into the street. She ducked behind her car as the front door of the building swung open.

She held her breath and peered over the front fender. The boys stepped out quickly, holding the stakes close to their sides. She saw Ross whisper something to Fletch. Fletch laughed and gave him a playful shove.

Dr. Weller backed out of the building. He locked the front door. Took several deep breaths, gazing around.

No. Please. Dad, please don't look here.

Hunched behind the car, Destiny watched them move quickly, silently up the sidewalk. She turned and saw her dad's SUV parked on the corner across the street.

Squatting low, Destiny moved to the other

side of her car. Another car passed by. Its head-lights spilled over the boys. Destiny saw them hide the wooden stakes so the driver wouldn't see.

They piled into the SUV. She watched her dad lower himself behind the wheel. He started it up. The taillights flared red. After a few seconds, the SUV pulled away from the curb.

Destiny jumped to her feet.

Where is Dad going? She fumbled for her car keys. Dropped them onto the sidewalk.

Trembling, she grabbed up the keys and hurried into the car. It felt good to sit down. Breathing hard, she started up the car and headed after them.

A few seconds later, she began to catch up. They were driving fast through North Town, the old part of Dark Springs. Small houses crowded together on tiny lots. An all-night gro-cery on one corner. A boarded-up movie theater.

Destiny hit the brake when she saw the SUV pull to the curb. The doors swung open, and the boys were out of the car before it even stopped.

Destiny swung the car over, her eyes on the boys. She bumped over the curb and bounced hard.

The boys were running across a narrow front lawn, leaping over the shrubs, moving silently, stakes raised high over their heads.

Whose house is this? I've been inside it. Isn't it the school librarian's house? Mrs. Lindros's?

The hunters' faces were hidden in shadow. But she could see their black silhouettes leaning forward as they ran.

Then she heard the shouts. Heard the crack of breaking glass. Heard heavy thuds as they broke the front door down.

Oh my God. Oh my God. I don't believe this. They're breaking in. My dad is breaking into a house. They're going in.

A few seconds later, she heard more shouts. And then a woman's high wail. A wail of pain, of horror.

Destiny covered her ears. But she couldn't shut out the terrifying cry.

I've got to get home. I've got to tell Livvy.

She wheeled the car around. Made a wild U-turn, nearly smashing into the side of a parked pickup truck. The squealing tires reminded her of the woman's high shriek.

My dad . . . my own dad . . .

What am I going to do?

* * *

She found Livvy lying on her bed, reading an issue of *People* magazine. "Where've you been?" Livvy asked coldly as Destiny hurried across the room to her.

"Listen to me. We—we're in trouble," Destiny cried.

Livvy rolled her eyes. "Tell me something I don't know."

Destiny dropped down on the edge of the bed. "You don't know *this*. Dad is a hunter. I saw him. I saw him tonight. Our own dad is a hunter."

The magazine fell from Livvy's hands. "Oh my God. That's impossible!"

Destiny took a deep breath. "It's true. I saw Ross and Fletch with him. And other guys from school. They broke into Mrs. Lindros's house."

"The librarian from school?"

Destiny nodded. "They killed her. I heard her scream. It was so horrible!"

Livvy pulled herself up. She shook her head hard. "Ross was there? With Dad?"

"Yes. I swear. They're both hunters."

"But Dad wouldn't hurt us. We're his daughters."

Destiny swallowed hard. "I don't know what he would do if he found out. He's been lying to us all this time. He said he was working late. But all the while, he's been a hunter."

Livvy tugged at a strand of hair. "I—I just can't believe it."

"You've got to stay away from Ross," Destiny said. "He's a hunter too."

"So what?" Livvy cried.

"So what? Have you lost your mind? If Ross found out our secret—"

"Ross would never hurt me," Livvy insisted. "Never. Ross loves me, Dee."

Destiny's voice came out in a shrill whisper. "Would he still care about you if he knew? Would he?"

"You're just jealous," Livvy said. "You're jealous that Ross is in love with me."

The words stung Destiny. "I'm not jealous. He's a hunter. And if he knew—"

"He already knows!" Livvy cried. "Ross already knows. I told him. He knows all about it."

"What? How could you?" Destiny screamed. "How could you put us both at risk? We swore to keep the secret. We swore to each other. How could you tell him?"

Livvy turned her face to the wall and didn't answer.

"When did you tell him? What did he say? Answer me," Destiny demanded. "Answer me, Livvy. What did he say?"

Livvy didn't move and didn't reply.

"Don't you realize what you've done?" Destiny cried. "Don't you realize the danger we're in now?"

Chapter Thirty-Six
Renz Makes a Promise

Destiny watched Renz walk down the hall. He appeared startled to see her, but a smile quickly replaced his surprise. "Good morning, Destiny. Waiting outside my office door? Hope you haven't been waiting long."

"I wanted to talk to you before school began."

He switched his briefcase to his other hand, pushed open the door, and waved her in before him. At his desk, he turned and smiled at her again, his dark eyes flashing. "You look tired. Are those lines under your eyes?"

"I didn't sleep much last night," Destiny said. "I was worried about coming here . . . about talking to you. I . . . well . . . this isn't easy."

His eyes burned into hers. "What's on your mind?"

Destiny stared back at him. "Well . . . I don't

really know how to say this." Her throat suddenly felt dry.

I can't do this. This is crazy. I should turn and run.

Renz leaned closer. His eyes caught the light. "Why don't you just say it? It can't be that difficult."

Yes, it is.

"Well . . ."

His eyes appeared to glow. He didn't blink. She suddenly felt as if he was reaching into her mind, reading her thoughts.

"You want to talk to me about the full moon, don't you?" he said softly.

Destiny gasped. He *did* read her mind.

She nodded.

"You're nervous about Saturday night," Renz said.

Destiny nodded again. "You know!" she whispered. "You . . . you *are* the Restorer—aren't you!"

He blinked. "The *what?*"

"The Restorer. It's you. You're the one who restores people to their normal lives after they've been bitten."

He didn't answer.

"Please, tell me, Renz." Her voice broke. "Tell me the truth. Are you the one? Are you the Restorer?"

Renz gazed at her for a long moment. He seemed to be thinking hard. Finally, a smile spread across his handsome face. He took Destiny's hand.

"Yes," he whispered. "Yes, I am."

His hand felt warm and dry on her cold hand. She let out a long sigh of relief. "Oh, thank God," she cried. "Livvy and I— we need you, Renz. We need you desperately. We don't have much time. Will you help us?"

He pressed her hand between both of his. He stood and came up close beside her. "Don't worry anymore," he whispered. "The full moon is Saturday night. I'll be there, at the senior overnight. I will come for you. And I promise I will take care of you then."

"Thank you. Oh, thank you," Destiny whispered.

Chapter Thirty-Seven
Summary Camp Memories

Destiny greeted Nakeisha at the front door, and the two girls hugged. Destiny led her friend into the living room. "You look great!"

Nakeisha spun around, modeling her outfit. She wore a white sweater vest over a silky orange top, a short brown suede skirt, and dark tights. "It's my college interview outfit. Check it out."

Destiny laughed as Nakeisha paraded back and forth like a model on a runway. "Hope you don't walk like that at your interviews. How's it going?"

Nakeisha shrugged. "Not bad. I've only seen a few schools. Mom wants me to stay in the east. She won't let me apply to any California schools."

Nakeisha's eyes narrowed on Destiny. "Have you lost weight?"

Destiny bit her bottom lip. "A little."

"Well, don't lose any more," Nakeisha said in her usual blunt way. "You look like we did after that two-day canoe trip. Wrecked."

"I . . . haven't been sleeping well," Destiny said, motioning for Nakeisha to sit on the green leather couch. "I don't know why. Senior-year-itis, I guess."

Nakeisha glanced around. "Nice house. Is Livvy home?"

Destiny dropped beside her on the couch. "No. I don't know where she is."

"Hope she comes by. I wanted to say hi to her."

"Livvy and I haven't been getting along." The words burst from Destiny's mouth. She hadn't intended to say them.

She didn't want to involve Nakeisha in her troubles. She didn't want to tell Nakeisha anything about what was going on.

"I'm not surprised," Nakeisha said. "You two are so different. It's hard to believe you're really twins."

"Well . . ." Destiny had the sudden urge to tell her friend everything. But she forced the words back.

"Hey, you know who I heard from?" Nakeisha asked. "Ronnie Herbert. Know what he's doing?"

Destiny shook her head. "I only got one e-mail from him, at the end of summer."

"You know how he was such a wizard with the camp computers? Well, he started his own computer repair business after school. You know. Doing upgrades for people, installing hardware, and stuff. He said he's making money big-time."

"Good for Ronnie," Destiny said, trying to sound enthusiastic.

"Hear from anyone else at camp? Oh, wait." Nakeisha jumped to her feet. "I forgot. Know what I brought?" She went to the front hall, rummaged in her bag, and pulled out a thin book. "Did you get this?"

"What is it?"

Nakeisha returned to the couch, holding the book up to Destiny. "It's the camp yearbook. It just came yesterday morning."

"I didn't get mine."

Nakeisha pushed it into Destiny's lap. "Well, check it out. Look. We're on the cover."

Destiny moaned. "Oh, great. That horrible day it rained like crazy. We look like drowned rats."

Destiny quickly turned the page. "There's the campfire from hell. I'll never forget those screaming little kids."

Nakeisha laughed. "Half of them wet their beds that night!"

"Hey, nice picture of Livvy," Destiny said, holding the book closer. "Who's that guy she's with?"

Nakeisha grabbed the book to study the photo. "What day was it taken? Livvy was going with a different boy every day, wasn't she? I mean, she didn't leave anyone for us."

Destiny's eyes rolled over the photos. "Oh, wow. This is great."

I wish I was back in camp. I wish I could turn the clock back . . .

"But do you know what's totally weird?" Nakeisha took the book and flipped quickly through the pages. "No photos of Renz. Not one."

Destiny's mouth dropped open. "Renz . . . ?"

"Go ahead. You look." Nakeisha shoved the book back onto Destiny's lap. "Renz was everywhere, right? He was in every activity. So how come they left him out of the yearbook?"

Destiny swallowed hard. She let the yearbook slide from her lap, onto the floor. "Renz? At camp? He's at my school. No way he was at camp."

"Huh? At your school?" Nakeisha jumped to

her feet again. She pressed her hands to her waist and frowned at Destiny. "Are you totally losing it? I'm talking about Renz. R-e-n-z. We hung out with Renz all summer. You panted after him and followed him around just like all us girls. Are you telling me you don't remember that?"

Destiny stared up at her friend. She suddenly felt dizzy. She gripped the side of the couch.

Renz at camp. Renz, the new college advisor from school, at camp. How can that be?

And suddenly, she saw herself with him. She and Renz at the lake . . . the full moon high above the shimmering water. Renz leaning over her . . . kissing her . . .

Oh my God.

Slowly, the truth began to filter into her spinning mind.

I get it. I get it now.

No pictures of Renz in the yearbook.

No memory of him at camp. But he was there. I knew him. I hung out with him. I . . . kissed him.

No pictures and no memories of him . . .

Vampires can't be photographed . . .

Renz is a vampire. Yes. It's so obvious now, thanks to Nakeisha and the yearbook. Renz is the vampire who ruined our lives.

"He's not the Restorer," she said, thinking out loud.

Nakeisha continued to stand over her. "What? You're not making any sense, Dee."

Oh, yes, I am.

Renz isn't the Restorer.

Nakeisha was talking, but Destiny couldn't hear her, her words drowned out by Destiny's terrifying realization.

Destiny pressed her hands to the sides of her face and shut her eyes. Renz isn't the Restorer. . . . My dad is a vampire hunter. . . . My closest friends are hunters too. My sister isn't speaking to me. After Saturday, I will be like Mrs. Bauer, a mad creature driven night and day by an endless craving for blood.

"Destiny? Are you freaking out or something? Are you okay?" Nakeisha's voice—far away, miles away—broke into her thoughts.

No. I'm not okay.

I'm not okay.

I have no one to turn to, no one I can trust.

Saturday night . . . Saturday night . . . Saturday night . . . my life will be over.

Part Five

Chapter Thirty-Eight
Renz Drinks Deeply

*R*enz sat at his desk, leaning back in his chair, eyes shut. "Destiny." He whispered her name. Thinking about Saturday night filled him with excitement. "Destiny . . . Laura. Yes, you will become Laura."

Memories flooded his mind. It was last spring . . . only last spring, but it seemed so long ago . . . when he spotted his love behind the high school, waiting for her daughters again. Yes, she called herself Deborah Weller, and she was married to a boring-looking veterinarian.

But I don't care what you call yourself. Tonight you will be Laura again, he thought, gazing up at the full moon. He let the moonlight warm him, then returned his eyes to her. He was afraid to let her out of his sight, afraid he might lose her.

Ever since that chance meeting in the school parking lot, he had been thinking about

Deborah Weller, following her, watching her. He would creep up to the kitchen window at night and watch the family eat their dinner. Through the window, he watched her and enjoyed her laugh, her smile, her bright green eyes.

Laura, do you sense that I am near?

Do you sense my love for you?

We are separated, Laura. But not for long.

And then, a few days later, Renz knew the time had come. The full moon sent silvery light over her SUV as she waited in the empty parking lot. He moved out of the shadows, toward the car, ready to claim his bride.

She had the windows closed. Her blond hair fell softly to her shoulders, caught in the light of the moon. He tapped lightly on her window and saw her jump in surprise.

She gazed out at him for a long moment, then remembered him. She rolled down the window. "Mr. Angelini? How strange. We keep meeting in this parking lot."

Her throaty voice, like velvet. Like Laura.

"Could you help me?" he asked, barely able to keep his voice from quivering. "I dropped my keys. If you open the door, the car light will help me find them."

She didn't hesitate. She opened the car door.

He reached in and grabbed her.

He held her so tightly, she couldn't scream.

At last. At last. *At last.*

The fangs slid down and he drove them deep into her throat. He drank hungrily, noisily, holding her powerless against him.

When he had drunk his fill, blood flowing over his lips and chin, he raised his head and whispered, "Now, you must drink, Laura. Now you must drink my blood."

He raised his throat to her. He could see the haze in those deep green eyes, the confusion on her face.

"Drink," he ordered. "Drink and we will be together."

She turned her head.

The doors to the school opened. The twins appeared.

No. Oh, no.

Renz loosened his grip. He backed away, then slithered into the shadows of the trees at the edge of the parking lot.

He watched the girls run to the car. Watched Laura mopping at her throat with the collar of her blouse. Covering up the wound. Greeting the girls. Confused. Dazed and unaware of what had just happened to her.

But I know what has happened, he thought. I have drunk your blood under the full moon, and now you need to drink mine. I need you. I need you.

The girls were inside the car now. He heard the click of the door locks. He waited until the car pulled away, out of the parking lot. And then he tilted back his head and uttered a long, animal howl, a howl of anger and frustration and pain.

The days went by. Renz knew he had to wait a month, until the next full moon. He watched her house. What was she doing in there? She seldom came out.

What did she tell her husband? Her daughters? That she was sick?

Evenings, he saw the husband returning from his veterinary lab. Renz saw what he brought for his wife. The husband brought animals home—rabbits, hamsters, small rodents. For his wife to feed upon?

So the husband knows, Renz decided. He brings her food. But he can do no more for her. He is powerless.

Only I can save you, Laura. Only I can return you to the life we planned so many decades ago.

The days and nights passed so slowly. The last winter storm gave way to warmer spring nights. Renz watched the moon, waiting.

At last, the full moon rose high over the trees. Laura's house stood dark except for a light in her bedroom. The twins had spring break and were away at a friend's. The little brother had gone to a sleepover a few blocks away. The husband worked late at his lab.

Renz knew all these things because he stayed close—close to the house and its inhabitants.

If I look away for a moment, she might disappear. And I might lose her again.

But no. The moon floated high and full, lighting the house like a spotlight. And Laura was in her bedroom.

Awaiting me.

He crept along the side of the house, pressing against the shingles, making his way to her room in the back. The bedroom window was open, curtains fluttering in the light breeze.

He hesitated for only a moment, pushing

back his excitement. But he could already taste her sweet blood on his tongue. And once their blood had mingled, he could picture her joy at being reunited with him.

He raised his hands to the windowsill and hoisted himself easily into her room. He pushed away the filmy curtains. A dim bed-table lamp provided the only light.

He stumbled back against the wall when he saw her, trying to blink the horrible sight away.

The sight of Deborah's body, dangling so stiffly from the ceiling light. Her bare feet floating above the floor. The thick rope around her neck. Her head tilted back, eyes staring blankly at the ceiling, her face blackened, purple tongue hanging from her open mouth.

"No!"

He spun to face the wall. He couldn't bear to see this.

Why did you do this, Laura? Why did you rob me once again of a bride?

He hunched there, facing the wall without moving for what seemed like hours. Finally, he moved to the window. "Farewell, Laura," he called softly. "Farewell. I have lost you once again."

He climbed out the window. He strode across the grass. He didn't look back. "You have escaped me. But you have two daughters. Two Lauras. You got away from me, Deborah. *But I will never let them go!*"

Chapter Thirty-Nine

Destiny Keeps Her Date With Renz

Ana-Li tossed a Frisbee to Destiny. It bounced off Destiny's outstretched hand and sailed into the side of a tent.

Ana-Li laughed. "I hope no one is in there."

Destiny loped over the grass, picked up the Frisbee, and spun it back to her friend. She gazed up at the rising full moon, already high in the purple night sky.

A shiver of fear ran down her back. I'm trying to pretend that everything is normal. But Ana-Li must see how distracted and frightened I am.

In the middle of the circle of tents, the campfire crackled and sent up sparks. Some kids were poking at it, trying to make it flame up. At the edge of the clearing, someone had cranked up a boombox, and several kids were dancing.

Away from the noise, a group of parents

and teachers—the chaperones—stood chatting near the lakeshore.

Ana-Li made a low toss, and the Frisbee rolled toward the fire. "We got such a beautiful night," she said. "Not a cloud in the sky."

Destiny muttered a reply. Her stomach gnawed. She fought back the hunger.

Soon I won't be able to control myself. Soon I won't be able to satisfy my craving. After tonight, Livvy and I will become creatures, creatures to be hunted down by my father and his hunters.

Destiny handed the Frisbee to Ana-Li. "I don't really feel like playing," she said. On the other side of the campfire, she saw Renz, surrounded by a group of girls, teasing them, everyone laughing, having a good time. Near the boombox, some girls were pulling Mr. Smith, the Spanish teacher, over to dance.

A sudden wind made the trees whisper. Destiny shivered again. She glimpsed her dad with the other parents at the shore.

Dad, if you only knew what was about to happen to your daughters . . .

"Everyone's trying really hard to have a good time," Ana-Li said. "I mean, it's the senior overnight and everything. But who really feels like partying that much? With two girls from our class dead . . . our two good friends . . ." Her voice trailed off.

Destiny sighed. "Senior year was supposed to be the best year of our lives. . . ."

Ana-Li glanced around the campground. "Where's your sister?"

Destiny shrugged. "We're sharing a tent, but I haven't seen her since we arrived. She's probably off in the woods with Ross. I don't see him, either."

Destiny's stomach growled. Her senses suddenly became sharp. She could hear the blood coursing through Ana-Li's veins. She could hear conversations on the other side of the campground. A babble of voices, all talking at once, all so loud in her ears.

"Think I'll get a hot dog or something," Ana-Li said. "Sure you don't want to come?"

"No, thanks." Destiny watched Ana-Li trot off to the food table. She turned and found Ari right behind her.

"Surprise!"

She jumped. "Hey, don't sneak up on me like that."

"Thought we were going to hang out tonight," he said.

Destiny had completely forgotten about him. "Yeah, I know. But—"

"There's a cool little dock on that side of the lake." He pointed. "Some kids are over there. You know. Partying."

"I don't think so," Destiny said. "I'm sorry, Ari. I . . . I'm feeling a little weird. I'm going to go lie down. In my tent."

His eyes flashed. "Can I join you?" He laughed. "Just kidding."

"Maybe I'll feel better later and I'll catch up to you," Destiny said. She could see the disappointment on his face.

"Okay. Catch you later," he said.

Maybe.

Maybe you'll see me and maybe you won't.

Maybe if you see me, you won't recognize me, Ari.

I did everything I could to find the Restorer. I worked so hard for Livvy and me. But I failed.

And now the moon is rising in the sky. Everyone thinks it's beautiful, the autumn full moon, so golden and big.

To me, it looks like death.

* * *

Her stomach gnawing, her throat aching with thirst, Destiny tried to bury herself inside her sleeping bag. But the tent walls were so thin and transparent that she could see the flickering light of the campfire through them. And the voices outside were loud. They seemed to be in the tent with her.

What time is it?

Will Renz really come for me when the moon is high?

She closed her eyes, but opened them when she heard the scrape of the tent flap.

She sat up slowly.

The tent flap opened, revealing the full moon high in the black sky.

And then, Renz poked his head in, blocking the moon, his eyes wide with excitement.

"Laura, it is time," he whispered. "I have come for you. Are you ready?"

"Yes," Destiny whispered. "I'm ready."

Chapter Forty

"At Last"

Leaning into the tent, Renz reached out his hand. Destiny grabbed it and allowed him to pull her to her feet.

"At last," he whispered, a smile spreading over his handsome face.

He led her out of the tent.

Destiny saw the orange embers of the dying campfire. They sent up red and yellow sparks like jewels into the night sky.

Renz held her in his arms. He pressed his mouth to her ear. "I've waited so long for this night."

Destiny's skin tingled. Her muscles tensed.

He lowered his face to hers. His fangs curled down from his gums. "Are you ready, Laura? Are you ready?"

"Yes," Destiny whispered. "Yes, yes . . ."

Then she grabbed the wooden tent pole she had placed beside the tent. Raised it high. And with a groan, shoved it deep into Renz's chest.

His eyes went wide and he uttered a startled hiss. He staggered back—

—and Destiny shoved the stake deeper.

"Oh, no. Oh, no," Renz whispered, arms flailing. He toppled to his back on the ground.

I planned this all week. It's all I could think about.

Now, die, Renz—die!

"Oh, no," he repeated. "You can't—" His arms and legs flailed like a pinned insect. "Laura, I love you. I love you, Laura."

He reached up and grabbed her by the shoulders. His bony fingers tightened, digging into her sweater, into her flesh. "I love you. I love you. . . ." He struggled to pull her down to him.

With a surge of strength, Destiny shoved the tent pole all the way through his body, into the ground.

Die, Renz—die!

A gurgling sound escaped from Renz's open mouth.

Destiny stared in horror as Renz's body began to fall apart. His arms and legs crackled and curled. The skin on his face melted away. His chest caved in. His skull disintegrated, leaving only his fangs.

In seconds, his clothing lay on the grass, empty, except for a few flakes of powdery dust that floated into the air.

Gasping for breath, Destiny spun away— and saw her father standing behind her.

"Destiny, I'm here," he whispered. "I saw—"

"Dad . . ." Destiny said, her entire body trembling. "Dad . . . I killed him. I had to. He . . . he came for me!" She pulled down the collar of her sweater and showed him the twin marks on her throat.

"No!" Dr. Weller let out a cry. He stared at her for a long moment, eyes wide with shock.

Then he grabbed the wooden stake from the ground and raised it high above his head.

"No!" Destiny screamed. "Dad, please don't! Don't hurt me!"

"Why didn't you tell me?" her father shouted. He heaved the stake across the field and wrapped Destiny in his arms. She could feel his hot tears on her cheek. "Dee, why didn't you tell me? I would never hurt you. Never!"

"Because . . ." She pulled away from him. "Because I know who you are, Dad. I know you're a hunter."

He shook his head. "Yes. Yes, I'm a hunter. But, Dee—I can help you. I have a cure."

She gazed up at him. "You . . . you're . . ."

He nodded. "Yes. I'm also the Restorer."

Chapter Forty-One
"I Guess I Should Tell You the Truth"

Dr. Weller grabbed Destiny's hand. He pulled her to his tent on the other side of the field. Safely inside, she dropped to her knees and watched him open his medical bag.

"What are you going to do, Dad?"

He bent over the bag. "I have a formula, Dee. It's taken me a long time, but I'm sure I finally have it right."

He held her arm and raised a hypodermic needle in his other hand. He searched for a vein, then plunged the needle into her arm.

The needle stung. "Will it really cure me?" she asked in a tiny voice.

He nodded, his face solemn. "It may not be instantaneous. But you will feel the symptoms begin to fade." Tears rolled down his cheeks. "I never dreamed I'd have to use it on my own daughter." He returned the needle to the bag.

Destiny felt a surge of heat roll through her body. The cure was right in my own house all along, she thought. "But—Dad, how did you find this? How can you do this?"

He squeezed her hand. He let out a long sigh. "Dee, there are so many things I've kept from you. I guess I should tell you the truth."

She stared at him. "The truth?"

"The truth about your mother . . ."

Destiny's throat tightened. "What about Mom?"

He took a deep breath. "You're not going to like what I have to say. I hoped never to have to tell you. You see . . . your mother was attacked by a vampire. It happened last year, at the end of the winter."

Destiny gaped at her father. "But . . . you said she committed suicide."

"Yes, she did. She couldn't bear the horror. After she was bitten, she started to change. We told you kids she was sick. There was no way we could tell you the truth."

"Oh my God," Destiny whispered. "Oh my God."

"I went to work in my lab," her father continued, holding her hand tightly. "I worked night and day. I knew I could find a cure with the research I'd been doing. But . . . I failed. I didn't find the cure in time. I failed, Dee. I felt so helpless, so miserable."

Destiny's head spun. "Mom? Attacked by a vampire? But, Dad, I can't believe it. I—"

"At first, she wasn't too bad. But her hunger grew. I tried to help. I brought lab animals home for her to feed on. But then the next full moon was approaching. She wasn't herself at all. She needed more and more blood. Her thirst for blood became so intense, she prowled at night. She didn't know what she was doing. She . . . she took more than one human victim."

Destiny gasped and shut her eyes. Not Mom . . . oh, no. Not Mom . . .

"This is so hard for me." Dr. Weller's voice broke. "How can I tell you all this? I—I can't live with it myself."

Destiny opened her eyes. "Go on, Dad. Please. I want to know the truth."

He took another breath. "Well . . . Coach Bauer's wife—poor Marjory—your mother's best friend, she was one of your mother's victims.

"After that, when your mother realized

what she had done to Marjory, she was over-come with horror and grief. She couldn't bear the guilt. She . . . she killed herself. She—"

He turned away from Destiny. She could see his shoulders trembling.

She stared at him, trying to digest all that he was telling her. "And that's why you became a vampire hunter?"

He turned back to her. "Yes. I tried to learn all that I could. I learned how to find vampires, how to hunt them, how to kill them. And all the while I worked in my lab—worked until I couldn't see straight—until I found a formula that could cure vampires who weren't entirely lost."

Destiny squeezed his arm. "But Mrs. Bauer—?"

"I tried, but I failed. Too much time had passed. I couldn't restore her. Poor Coach. He begged me to end her misery. He couldn't do it himself. So I came with my helpers and I did it."

A sob escaped his throat. "I've lived with such horror. I didn't want you to know any of it. I—"

"Oh my God! Livvy!" Destiny cried, jump-ing to her feet. "Dad—Livvy too! Livvy was bitten too. I can't believe I forgot her. We have to find her—fast!"

He shoved a flashlight into Destiny's hand. Then he latched his medical bag and picked it up. "My poor girls. My poor girls. Hurry. Let's go."

They searched the campground, then the lakefront.

Please let her be okay, Destiny thought. Please let us be in time to save her.

They stepped into the woods, following the circle of light from the flashlight. The full moon shone brightly overhead, making the tree leaves glimmer like silver. Somewhere, a night dove cooed, sweetly, calmly.

Livvy, where are you?

Livvy, don't hide from us.

They cleared their own path through the trees and the brambled weeds. The flashlight flickered, threatened to die, then revived.

Destiny gasped when she saw Livvy and Ross at the edge of a narrow, grassy clearing. They were both on their knees, bent over a fallen deer.

Dr. Weller's light swept over them.

Livvy and Ross slowly raised their heads from the deer. Their faces dripped with bright blood.

"Go away!" Livvy rasped. "Can't you see we're hungry?"

Chapter Forty-Two
Vanished

Destiny froze. "Livvy—no," she choked out. "You don't have to do this. Dad is the Restorer. Dad can cure you both."

Ross blinked several times as if dazed. Then he lowered his face into the torn belly of the deer. He began to drink, making loud sucking sounds.

Livvy stared at Destiny and her father defiantly. "We don't *want* to be cured," she shouted. "Ross and I—we made our choice. We want to be together—forever."

"Livvy, don't do this!" Dr. Weller shouted. "There might still be time. If you let me—"

Destiny strode up to the deer. "Let Dad try," she told her sister. "Maybe he can cure you. You have to let him try!"

"We're a family!" Dr. Weller cried, tears staining his cheeks. "Livvy, we're a family. We need you. We need you with us."

"It's too late!" Livvy screamed. "I've been an immortal *since camp*!"

"No!" Destiny gasped.

"Renz drank my blood and I drank his," Livvy rasped, blood dripping down her chin. "I didn't want to die like Mom. I couldn't stand the idea of death, of lying under the ground forever like Mom. I wanted to live forever—and Renz gave me the chance."

Destiny shook her head, trying to think clearly. "But you and I, Liv, we—"

"I'm sorry, Destiny. I'm so sorry. I didn't want to be his Laura. But I didn't know he would go after you. When we returned home, I only pretended to be a neophyte," Livvy said, her eyes wild, locked on her sister. "I only pretended to be frightened about what was happening, Dee. Didn't you wonder why I never helped you search for the Restorer? I already had my new life—my *immortal* life, and I was happy. And I thought you could learn to be happy too."

"No, Livvy. No!"

"And tonight Ross and I exchanged blood," Livvy said, grabbing Ross's hand. "Our blood mingled under the full moon. We did it, Dee.

Because we want to be together—forever!"

"No! No! I can't let you do this," Destiny cried, staggering up to the fallen deer. "You're my sister. My twin!"

A strange smile played over Livvy's blood-stained face. "Maybe you won't want me for a sister when I tell you the rest. I was the one who killed Bree and Courtney. I didn't want to. They were my friends. But what could I do? I couldn't fight my hunger. I had to feed. I had no choice. I killed them both."

"No!" Destiny screamed. "No. Please—no! You're lying. Please—tell me you're lying!"

Behind her she glimpsed her dad, fumbling in his medical bag. He pulled out a hypodermic needle. "Maybe there's still time," he shouted. "We're a family, Livvy. We're a family. Think of Mikey, how much he needs you. Please—I need you too."

Destiny took a deep breath. Then she dove over the side of the dead deer, sliding on the blood-soaked fur. She reached for Livvy with both hands. "I won't let you get away. I won't!"

Livvy jerked back—and Destiny toppled into the wet, pulpy open stomach of the deer.

She looked up in time to see Livvy and Ross

begin to change. Their bodies folded in on themselves. Their bones crackled. Their faces disappeared.

They rose over the fallen deer as blackbirds, wings spread, flapping gently, catching the wind.

Dr. Weller sank to his knees. The needle fell from his hand. *"Noooooooo."* He buried his face in his hands.

Destiny watched the birds take off, two winged shadows over the full moon. Then they were gone . . . vanished into the black sky.

"Destiny?"

She heard a voice behind her. She turned to find Ari running into the clearing. "Destiny? Are you okay? I checked your tent, and you weren't there."

"Oh, Ari," she uttered. She threw her arms around his neck and began to sob.

Epilogue

Destiny slept uncomfortably, rolling over, bunching up her pillow, tossing off the covers. Six weeks after Livvy had left—and Destiny couldn't sleep without dreaming about her.

I don't want to sleep because then I have the nightmares.

But I'm so exhausted. I need to sleep.

"Dee?" A tiny voice at her ear.

She raised her head and realized that Mikey had climbed into bed with her. "Dee? Are you awake?"

"Uh-huh." She squinted at him.

"I can't sleep." He snuggled against her. "I keep dreaming about Livvy."

"Me too," she whispered.

He was silent for a moment. Then, "Is it true? She's never coming back?"

Destiny sighed. "I don't know, Mikey. I really don't. All we can do is hope. . . ."

She sat up when she heard a tapping sound. At the window?

Yes. Tapping and fluttering.

Mikey stood up. Destiny climbed out of bed after him. They hurried to the window.

A clear, moonlit night. Everything so still.

And then a bird flew up against the window glass. "A blackbird," Destiny whispered.

Mikey trembled beside her. She slipped her arm around his shoulders.

The bird hovered outside the window. Wings spread high, it floated on the other side of the glass, peering in . . .

. . . peering in longingly . . .

. . . with Livvy's green eyes.

"It . . . wants to come in," Mikey whispered.

Destiny hesitated. A chill ran down her back.

She stared into the bird's green eyes.

"Open it," Mikey whispered. "Let it in, Dee."

Destiny reached for the window.

But the blackbird turned and flew off into the night.

From *Dangerous Girls Two:*
The Taste of Night

Chapter One
My Sister is a Vampire

As Destiny Weller made the turn onto Collins Drive, a light rain started to fall. She squinted through the windshield, through the tiny, shimmering droplets of water, and pressed her cell phone to her ear.

"I think it's going to get really stormy," she said, glancing up at the lowering, black clouds. "I really don't feel like going out tonight, Ana-Li."

Her friend Ana-Li May made disappointed sounds at the other end. "I know it's hard for you, Dee. But the summer is going fast, you know. You should try to have at least a *little* fun."

Fun? How could she be talking about fun?

Destiny clicked on the headlights. The wipers left a smear on the windshield glass. She kept forgetting to replace the blades.

Hard to think about things like that.

"You've been really great," she told Ana-Li. "I mean, all summer. You're the only one who knows the truth about Livvy. I mean, except for Dad and Mikey. And Ari, of course. And you've been—OH!"

Destiny let out a cry. The cell phone fell from her hand as she hit the brakes hard. Her tiny, silver-gray Civic skidded on the wet pavement.

Startled by the sound, the girl on the sidewalk whipped her head around. Her face came into view.

Destiny gasped. No. Wrong again.

A car honked behind her. Heart pounding, she lowered her foot on the gas pedal and fumbled for the phone.

She could hear Ana-Li on the other end. "What's wrong? Dee? Are you okay?"

"Sorry." She leaned forward to squint through the smeared windshield. The rain pattered down harder. "I keep losing it. Every time I see a girl with long blond hair, I think it's Livvy."

"That's why you've got to get out of yourself," Ana-Li said. "You know. Go out. We'll go to a club or something. Dance our asses off.

Maybe meet some hot guys. It'll take your mind off . . . everything."

"*How can I take my mind off it?*"

She didn't mean to scream, but the words burst out of her in a shrill, trembling voice. "Ana-Li, my twin sister is a *vampire*! She's out flying around, prowling at night, hungry for warm blood, killing—killing things. I . . . I don't know what she's doing. I haven't seen her in two months. Do you know what that's done to my family? To my dad? My poor little brother?"

"Yes, of course I know, Dee. You don't have to scream at me. I—"

"There's *no way* I can take my mind off it," Destiny continued. She made a sharp right, tires skidding again. She'd almost missed her turn. "I think about Livvy all the time. And Ross too. I still can't believe he went with her. Ana-Li, I . . . I want to see Livvy. I just want to hug her. I know it's impossible, but I want to tell her to come back to us."

There was silence at Ana-Li's end.

"Ana-Li? Are you still there?"

"Yeah. I just don't know what to say. You know, I'll be leaving for orientation. Yale is a long way from here. I thought maybe in the short time we have . . ."

Destiny pulled into a parking spot at the curb in front of the familiar, low redbrick building. The rain had slowed. The wipers left a thick, gray smudge as they scraped over the glass.

That's the way I see everything these days, Destiny thought bitterly. Through a dark blur.

"Listen, Ana-Li. I have to go. I'm here, at my dad's office. I have to pick him up because his SUV broke down again. He never takes care of it." She sighed. "He can't seem to take care of anything these days. Just stays in his lab twenty hours a day. Then he comes home too wrecked to talk or do anything."

"Sorry," Ana-Li murmured on the other end.

"No, *I'm* sorry," Destiny said. "Here I am, laying all this on you again for the hundredth time. I'm really sorry. Can I call you later?"

"Yeah. Sure."

She clicked the phone shut and dropped it into her bag. Then she took a deep breath while checking her short, blond hair in the mirror.

Ana-Li has been terrific, she thought. She's always been a great friend. After that horrible night Livvy and Ross decided they wanted to live forever as vampires . . . Ana-Li has always been there for me.

She slid out of the car and gazed up at the sign above the glass door: WELLER VETERINARY CLINIC. Yes, her dad still treated sick cats and dogs, spayed and neutered them, gave them their shots, washed away their fleas, and mended their broken bones. But he spent most of his time in his lab at the back of the building, reading, studying old books, mixing chemicals, working out endless equations, searching for a cure for vampirism.

Destiny made her way through the brightly lit waiting room, empty now, quiet except for the gurgling sounds from the fish tank in the wall. "Hey, Dad—are you ready?" Her voice echoed down the hall as she passed the empty examining rooms.

"Dad?"

She found him hunched over the worktable in the lab, surrounded by darkness, standing under a cone of light from the single ceiling lamp. His eyeglasses reflected the light. He didn't seem to hear her at first.

"Dad? I'm here."

To her surprise, he had tears running down his cheeks. He crumpled the papers in his hand, then furiously ripped them in half and sent them flying to the floor.

"Dad—?"

Dr. Weller turned to Destiny, his face flushed, his eyes hidden behind the shiny glasses. "I'm afraid I have very bad news," he said.

Chapter Two

"Can You Kill Your Own Daughter?"

Destiny's breath caught in her throat. "Dad—what is it?" she finally choked out. She hurried across the room and stood across the table from him, under the bright, white light.

He shook his head. "It's my work. It's going nowhere. I'm no closer to finding a cure than I was two months ago."

Destiny grabbed the edge of the metal table with both hands. "But you'll keep trying, right, Dad? I mean, you're not giving up, are you?"

His pale blue eyes stared at her from behind his glasses, thick gray eyebrows arching high on his balding head. "I don't know how much time I have." His voice came out in a whisper. His eyes didn't move from Destiny's. "I'm under a lot of pressure."

"Pressure? I don't understand, Dad."

He stepped around the table and put an arm around her shoulders. "A lot of pressure." He hugged her briefly, then guided her to his small office at the side of the lab.

He dropped heavily into his desk chair, brushing back the tuft of gray hair on top of his head. Destiny stood, tense, in front of the desk, arms crossed over the front of her blue T-shirt.

"You know I have chosen two roles," Dr. Weller said, gazing up at her. "I'm the Restorer, the one who can restore neophyte vampires to their normal lives, if they're not already complete vampires."

I know very well, Destiny thought with a shiver. You don't have to explain, Dad. You restored *me*, remember? I was bitten too, just like Livvy. But you restored me, and now I'm fine, perfectly normal. But Livvy . . .

"And I'm also the Hunter," her dad continued, breaking into her thoughts. "Ever since your mother died . . . killed herself because of a vampire . . . I . . . I . . . I've vowed to kill as many vampires as I can. To rid Dark Springs of this . . . this filthy plague."

He rubbed his chin. Destiny saw that he hadn't shaved for at least a day or two. "My two roles . . . curing and hunting . . . they don't always go together."

"What do you mean, Dad? Destiny lowered herself into the wooden armchair across from the desk. "What's going on?"

"I've been working so hard to find a cure," he said. "You know. A cure for Livvy. And for Ross too. And any other vampire who wants it. And I've been neglecting my duties as a hunter."

Destiny leaned forward, her hands tightly clasped. All her muscles tensed as her father went on.

"The vampires in this town . . . they've become an even bigger danger. There are too many of them. People are starting to become aware . . ."

Destiny swallowed. "You mean, that couple that was murdered in Millerton Woods last weekend?"

Dr. Weller nodded. "The police have been able to keep everything quiet. People in Dark Springs don't know about the vampires. Like your friends, Dee. Your friends all think that Livvy and Ross ran away together. They . . . they don't know the truth."

Destiny nodded. "Just Ana-Li knows. And Ari, because he was there that night. No one else."

Dr. Weller frowned, deep lines creasing his forehead. "Well, people are starting to guess. The police have been getting calls. Mayor Hambrick has been getting frightened calls. He wants to get the governor to call in the National Guard. I can't let that happen. Too many innocent people will be killed."

"What are you going to do?" Destiny asked.

"I have no choice. I have to get my hunters together. I have to hunt them down—and kill as many vampires as I can."

Destiny let out a sharp cry. "Kill them?"

She suddenly pictured Livvy . . . Livvy before this all happened . . . when their mother was still alive. Livvy in that sexy red halter dress she wore to the spring dance their junior year. Her hair all shimmering, cascading down her bare back. The bright red lipstick . . . her sparkly earrings . . . her smile . . .

Destiny shook herself to chase the picture away.

"You can't just go out and kill vampires," she told her father. "How will you find them?"

Dr. Weller leaned forward over the desk. He grabbed Destiny's hands and held them between his. "There's an abandoned apartment building across the river from the campus. It was supposed to be student housing, a dorm for the community college. But the construction company went bankrupt and the building was never finished."

Destiny narrowed her eyes at him. "And—?"

"We think several vampires are using that building. Sleeping there during the day. Living in the apartments. I have my hunters organized. We're going there. Going into those apartments and killing as many of them as we can."

Destiny pulled her hands free. She jumped to her feet. "When? When are you doing this?"

"In two weeks—the next full moon."

Destiny swallowed, her throat suddenly dry. "Two weeks!"

He nodded. "Yes. We'll go in at sunrise when they're all asleep. I wanted to warn you. I mean, if something happens to me . . ." His voice trailed off.

"But, Dad—" Destiny realized she was shaking. "What about Livvy? What if Livvy is in one of those apartments? You . . . you can't kill your own daughter. You can't!"

A sob escaped Dr. Weller's throat. "My daughter is already dead."

Destiny moved around the desk and grabbed her father's sleeve. "But she's not! She's still alive. You know she's not dead. You can't do it. You can't kill her—*can* you?"

"I don't know!" Dr. Weller hugged Destiny again and held her tight. "I don't know. I don't know! If I find Livvy in there . . . I don't know what I'll do."

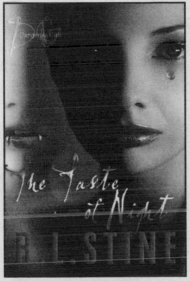